HEALING TIME

The Comanche bullet had done Skye Fargo a lot of damage. It had torn away the flesh on his shoulder, and let the blood pour out as from a spigot. He'd pitched forward face-first in the dust, and come to as weak as a cat.

But a couple of days had passed since then, and when he looked at Rita Mendoza, he didn't feel weak at all.

"I've been wondering," he said to her. "That time we had back at your place in Bent Rock. That wasn't all fake."

She laughed huskily and tipped her head back against a boulder. "For a while it was," she admitted. "But then my body, it take over. That I could not fake."

He chuckled. "That's for sure."

"You not get no ideas now," she warned him quickly. "You still sick man."

Skye didn't bother to argue. He just pulled away the blanket that covered him to prove otherwise.

Rita followed his gaze—and stopped arguing, too. . . .

Exciting Westerns by Jon Sharpe from SIGNET

(0451)

THE TRAILSMAN 46

HELL TOWN

by
Jon Sharpe

A SIGNET BOOK

NEW AMERICAN LIBRARY

PUBLISHER'S NOTE

This novel is a work of fiction. Names, characters, places, and incidents either are the product of the author's imagination or are used fictitiously, and any resemblance to actual persons, living or dead, events, or locales is entirely coincidental.

The Trailsman

Beginnings . . . they bend the tree and they
mark the man. Skye Fargo was born when he
was eighteen. Terror was his midwife, vengeance his first cry. Killing spawned Skye
Fargo, ruthless, cold-blooded murder. Out of
the acrid smoke of gunpowder still hanging
in the air, he rose, cried out a promise never
forgotten.

The Trailsman, they began to call him, all
across the West: searcher, scout, hunter, the
man who could see where others only looked,
his skills for hire but not his soul, the man
who lived each day to the fullest, yet trailed
each tomorrow. Skye Fargo, the Trailsman,
the seeker who could take the wildness of a
land and the wanting of a woman and make
them his own.

1861 ... Texas, its men off fighting for the Confederacy, leaving its ranches and livestock ripe plumbs for a renegade band of Comancheros

1

Peering through the heat, Fargo could see the small house below him, the familiar barn and the trees becoming more solid with each passing moment as the pinto carried him over the ridge down into the lush grasslands of the river bottom. He could see clearly as well the fat, sleek horses grazing below him on both sides of the river and the crowd of horses in the corral behind the barn.

He was pleased. Conchita Alvarez was doing well.

Reaching the bottom land, he felt at once the refreshing coolness welling up from the deep, moist grasses swelling about him, and a moment later, his Ovaro's hooves sending up gleaming shards of spray, he splashed across the river and rode straight for the house and barns. Dismounting to one side of the small log ranch house, he led the pinto into the shade of a cottonwood, dropped his reins over a low branch, then strode over to the porch and mounted it, his heavy boot heels echoing sharply in the quiet afternoon.

Before he reached the door, it was flung open, and Conchita—her eyes wide with delight—appeared in the doorway.

"Skye!" she cried.

Fargo stepped forward and wrapped both arms around her, his hat falling off in his enthusiasm. Flinging her arms around his neck, Conchita planted her full lips eagerly upon his. After a long kiss, she stepped back, surveying him up and down.

"You son of a bitch! You finally come back!"

Fargo grinned and picked up his hat. "Told you I would."

"I never believe you," she cried. "By God, I never believe no man, 'specially no gringo."

He reached for her again, but she shook her head emphatically. "You are dirty and need shave, Skye Fargo. Get in here!" Taking his hand, she pulled him in after her and proceeded to poke wood into the stove's belly, preparatory to building a fire.

Watching her, Fargo chuckled. "Some greeting!" he told her, slumping into a big, familiar chair. "First thing you do when you see me is heat water for my bath. What've you got to wash the dust off my tonsils?"

"Aha!" she cried. "I have just the thing." Hurrying over to the cupboard beneath the sink, she produced a bottle of bourbon and held it up for him to see.

Handing him the bottle and a tin cup, she vanished

outside, to return a moment later with a bucket full of water.

"How you like that?" she asked him as he filled his cup a second time.

"You must've known I was coming," he said, stoppering the bottle and placing it down on the floor beside him.

She poured the water into a kettle sitting on the stove. "It is not that, Skye. A woman get thirsty, too. And the nights, they are long and cold."

"Not anymore, Conchita. Not for a while, anyway."

She looked over at him and smiled, its warmth almost melting him. "I like hear you say that, Skye."

"Just get that water heated, Conchita. We got things to do."

She laughed and hurried out for more water, as anxious as he was for their bodies to get reacquainted.

With a soft cry, Conchita dug her fingernails into his back. Fargo laughed huskily and continued to thrust as she grabbed him more firmly, pressing her heels into the back of his legs. Her cheeks were flushed, her features almost rock-hard by now, her eyes half-opened slits watching him, her nostrils flared. He continued thrusting solidly, driving into her with long, deep strokes. Suddenly she flung her head back as a shudder raced through her body. She compressed her lips and closed her eyes.

As the fluid warmth of her orgasm took hold of him, he lost all sense of deliberation and, still thrusting, followed after her over the edge. A moment later, as their breathing subsided, she combed his damp hair back off his forehead with long, gentle fingers.

"Kiss me," she breathed, her tongue moistening her lips eagerly. "Kiss me again, Skye."

As he bent to kiss her, he heard the pinto standing outside at the hitch rack whinny softly, irritably. He paused, chiding himself. He had left the Ovaro to stand all this time, still fully saddled.

"What is eet?" Conchita asked, her dark hand reaching out to restrain him. "You have just begun, is it not so?"

He leaned down and kissed her full, passionate lips. "That's right, Conchita. But my horse. I haven't taken off his saddle yet."

"You have been here only a little while."

He smiled. "But this time I plan to stay awhile, Conchita. I'm gettin' sick of chasing all over hell and back for them two bastards. Maybe it's time I settled down for a spell."

"Ah! You make my heart sing. Go now. See to your beeg, fine pony. Then come back here where I wait for you."

Fargo stood up and pulled his buckskin pants on. As he did so, he looked down at Conchita as she lay shamelessly on her back, a fine film of sweat causing her lush body to glow softly. One look at her and there was no doubt in Fargo's mind she had been worth the long ride south.

Her breasts were like melons, the areolae around each nipple dark and large, the nipples themselves big enough to fill a grown man's mouth. Maybe her hips were too large by some men's standards, but not by

Fargo's. They were ample and rounded, a perfect saddle for a man as large and powerful as he. Her thick, powerful thighs, as strong as tree limbs, could hold a man and drive him deep and keep him there. But more than that. She was all woman. No pretense. No coquettish games. A she-cougar in the sack, and a fine cook and housekeeper on her feet.

He reached over and slapped her round tummy, then tickled her luxuriant muff of pubic hair. "I won't be long."

She pouted. "Hurry back, Fargo. Already I am restless for you."

The sun hit him like a hammer. He winced and pulled his hat brim down over his eyes as he walked over to the cottonwood to get the pinto. He found a stall in the rear, backed the pinto in, then stepped in beside the handsome black-and-white Ovaro, and unsaddled him. Peeling off the saddle blanket, he wiped off the rivulets of sweat that stood on the pony's back, then dried him off. He was setting down a full water bucket in front of the stall when he felt rather than heard the presence of someone moving up behind him.

He started to turn. Something heavy and unyielding crunched down onto the top of his head. He lost consciousness so quickly he never remembered hitting the barn floor.

What awoke him was the awful stench of smoke. He sat up and saw a blazing beam wrenching loose over his head. He rolled out of the way as the beam smashed into an empty stall beside him, igniting the

13

stall and the hay in it. The lofts above were blazing, as were most of the other stalls. The pinto was flinging wildly about in his stall, whinnying in terror, his heels smashing at the sides gate.

Jumping to his feet, Fargo raced over to the stall, doused the saddle blanket with the bucket of water sitting beside it, then draped the blanket over the pinto's head. The rear of the barn had already fallen away, the flames devouring its dry, weathered boards. Fargo pulled the terrified pinto through this gaping hole, then yanked off the blanket and released the horse into the corral.

That was when he heard Conchita's screams. The cabin, too, was being devoured by flames. Racing around the barn, Fargo saw the small cabin close to collapsing. As he headed toward the blazing building, he heard the thunder of many hooves off to his right, and glancing over, he saw at least fifteen riders galloping off, driving before them Conchita's stock and two wagonloads of loot. From their dress and appearance, he knew at once they were Comancheros.

Reaching what was left of the cabin, he lowered his shoulder and burst through the front door. Momentarily halted by a thick wall of smoke and flame, he put his head down and crashed into the bedroom. It was not easy to make Conchita out through the smoke and flame of the burning mattress, but when he reached the bed, he winced and had to force himself to look at her.

He picked up her charred body and hurled himself through the window, coming down hard in the midst of shattered glass and window sash, his clothes smoking, his boots on fire. As he kicked off his boots and tried to beat out the flames, the roof collapsed. Blazing embers and great tongues of flame leapt into the sky. The heat beat upon him with searing fists, and as flaming beams and shingles showered down around him, he picked Conchita up and ran with her to the protection of the cottonwoods.

As he put her down, she gasped painfully and opened her eyes. "The pain," she whispered fiercely, "it is too much."

"You're hurt," Fargo admitted miserably. "Hurt bad, Conchita."

"Eet is all right, Skye," she told him, reaching out to comfort him. "Soon I will feel nothing more."

Fargo felt a terrible helplessness as he looked down at her smoking body and saw what the flames had done to her lovely hair, to the smooth sheen of her face and arms.

"Who were they?" he asked, leaning close. "Did you recognize any of them?"

"Yes," she hissed. "I know them! Comancheros led Hank Fletcher's! He . . . want me for his bed. I spit in his ugly face. So now . . . he do thees thing."

Fargo looked down into her large, magnificent eyes—mirrors now of incredible pain. "Tell me where I can find him."

"Sawtooth Range. He have place . . . Hell Town, they call eet." Then, grabbing his arm, she pleaded, "You weel get him for me, Fargo. Please! Make heem burn, too."

"Yes, Conchita," he told her grimly, "I will."

15

She managed a smile. Her eyes lit with sudden defiance. "Good! Now my soul rest in peace."

Her head fell back. Fargo leaned over her and rested his ear against her seared breast. He could find no heartbeat. Conchita was gone.

The Trailsman got to his feet and looked for a long, bitter moment down at Conchita's charred remains, then turned his head to look in the direction the fleeing Comancheros had taken. They were only a fading dust cloud now, but that didn't matter. He'd catch up to them.

Then he would make them burn, too.

2

The war cry came from beyond the next ridge.

Leaning over his pinto's straining neck, Fargo spurred him on up the steep slope. Topping the ridge a second later, he saw, in a flat below him, four Kiowa about to plunder a small covered wagon pulled up alongside a stream. An old-timer was trying to face down the encircling savages. Three of them were on foot, the fourth Kiowa was still astride his pony.

As Fargo raced down through a thick stand of pine toward the flat, he heard another war cry. He saw through the trees a Kiowa brave fall back as the old man flung him away from his wagon. At that moment, Fargo charged from the pines and fired a shot into the air, hoping to discourage the Kiowas.

The Indians froze for an instant as they saw him approaching. But when the mounted Kiowa saw that Fargo was alone, he uttered a fierce war cry, flung his pony around, and raced up the slope to meet Fargo's charge.

Galloping hard, Fargo fired at him, but his shot went wild. Another shot had no more luck, and by that time the Kiowa brave was on him. Driving his pony directly at the pinto, the brave forced Fargo to veer aside. The two horses collided. The Kiowa's war hatchet sliced down, glancing off Fargo's shoulder. He spun away from it and toppled from his pinto, coming down hard on the uneven ground. He rolled for a few feet until he came up hard against the side of a boulder.

Dazed, Fargo shook his head and peered up at the brave, a young buck eager to prove himself. Fargo's six-gun had gone flying when the two horses collided. He could see it lying on the ground beyond the boulder, impossible for him to reach now. Still somewhat dazed, Fargo pushed himself erect, spread his legs wide to balance himself, and waited for the mounted Kiowa's charge. The savage had slowed up, turned his mount, and put aside his war club. With a sudden series of high, keening cries, the Kiowa brave charged Fargo, holding his elaborately carved coup stick like a lance.

"A-he!" the brave shouted. "A-he! I claim it!"

Fargo knew what the brave was shouting. He was now about to touch his enemy with his coup stick in front of witnesses who could testify to his valor. Already, the other three Kiowa braves had remounted and were charging up the slope to witness the action.

But Fargo had no intention of allowing such a triumph for the Kiowa brave. Fargo's head cleared at the sight of the charging Kiowa. At the last moment, as the Indian leaned far out with his coup stick to tap Fargo on the head, he reached up quickly and snatched the stick's beaded haft with both hands. Then, planting his feet firmly, he leaned back and yanked hard as the brave swept past.

Lifted from his pony's back, the brave went sailing over Fargo's head. Throwing down the coup stick, Fargo raced around the boulder and snatched up his Colt, then spun to face the Indian, who had landed on his feet like a great cat. Ignoring the other warriors circling them, Fargo covered the young brave with his Colt.

The unhorsed Kiowa straightened defiantly and folded his arms, daring Fargo to shoot. Impressed, Fargo smiled at the brave, dropped his six-gun back into his holster, and held up his hand, palm out, in the time-honored sign for peace. The Kiowa was momentarily stymied, but a sudden shout of laughter from the mounted Kiowas circling them seemed to take the starch out of him. He flung Fargo an angry glance, then swung up onto his horse.

Fargo handed the brave his coup stick.

This brought another bark of laughter from the young Kiowa's companions. Then the four warriors wheeled their horses and galloped off. Reaching down for his hat, Fargo watched them gallop off for a moment, then remounted his pinto and rode on down the slope to the wagon.

The old-timer was busy putting back into his wagon the goods the Kiowas had spilled out onto the ground.

As Fargo approached, he paused and wiped his bewhiskered face with a red bandanna. He had a powerful gut that sagged over his belt, and broad yellow braces swelling over the blue cotton shirt he wore. But the man did not look soft, and quite likely wasn't.

When Fargo pulled to a halt beside the wagon, the old man grinned up at him. "Light and set a spell," he offered. "I don't have no fire goin' yet, but I'll kindle one soon enough. And I got plenty of coffee."

Fargo dismounted. "Anything liquid you might have handy—aside from water—would do nicely."

The old-timer reached into the back of his wagon and produced a fifth of bourbon and handed it to Fargo, who unstoppered it, wiped off the neck with his palm, and tipped it up. After varnishing his tonsils thoroughly, he handed back the bottle to the old-timer.

"Thanks."

"It's me who should be thankin' you," the man said. "That was right smart, not shooting that Kiowa buck down in his tracks. Made them respect you all the more after you unhorsed him." He stuck out his hand. "My name's Kettle, Charlie Kettle."

"Fargo," the Trailsman responded, shaking the man's hand. He found the old man's grip warm and powerful. "Skye Fargo."

Fargo helped the man clean up the area, then relaxed as Charlie Kettle built a fire in front of a log, emptied some Arbuckle into the pot, and planted it on the blazing flames. Then he took out a clay pipe, tamped in some tobacco, sat down on the log, and began drawing the fragrant smoke into his lungs.

Fargo sat down beside him and lit a cigar with a faggot from the fire. He had noticed the mining tools stashed in the wagon and asked Kettle if he was prospecting.

"What else'd I be doin' in this wasteland of rock and scrub?" he demanded cheerfully. "I don't expect to find too much pay dirt, just enough to keep me in tobacco and pancakes." He turned to face Fargo. "Life ain't worth much more than that."

"Pancakes and coffee?" Fargo asked, amused. "That all?"

"Think it over, Skye. Is anything else worth the bother?"

Fargo shrugged.

"That war party was sure disappointed when they pawed through the wagon and found only picks and shovels and my placer rocker. They was lookin' for mirrors and trinkets. And weapons."

"And liquor."

"Yep, but I keep that bottle well hidden—inside a panel over the wheel, right beside my Walker."

"Smart."

"Maybe so, maybe not. Them Kiowa devils was so disappointed, they was ready to start ripping me up one side and down the other—till you showed up. I'm much obliged. Most varmints in this neck of the woods would've gone the other way soon's they saw my trouble."

"Maybe."

"Ain't no maybe about it. By grannies, the human animal is as foul a beast as any that ever set foot on this planet. And that's the God's truth. And women, they is even worse." He removed the pipe stem from his mouth and spat emphatically. "They is the devil's creations, sent here to tear a man's heart from his breast, then stomp it into the dust—grinnin' all the while."

Fargo smiled. He was enjoying Kettle's bombast.

"I been married six times. I give them devils' apprentices all the chances I could. And there weren't one didn't do me in, or try to."

Fargo puffed on his cigar, deciding against asking Charlie why it took him six marriages to learn his lesson.

Charlie leaned over and lifted the steaming coffeepot off the fire, then poured out the black liquid into the two tin cups he had set out. "What brings you into Arizona Territory, Skye?" he asked, handing Fargo one cup.

Skye told him about Conchita and the fire.

"Thought so," said Charlie, shaking his head dubiously. "A woman's behind it. A woman's behind every good thing a man does—and every fool thing. Never seed it to fail."

"I want that son of a bitch Hawk Fletcher."

"You ain't the only one."

"You know the man?"

"Not well enough to stand him to a drink. But I know him well enough. Hell, this entire territory knows him."

"What can you tell me?"

"First off, you know how these here Comancheros got this here treaty with the Comanches that allows them to trade with them and act as a go between."

Fargo nodded.

"Well, now that the Texans and other militia have left to fight that war in the East, this feller Hawk has taken over the Comancheros. He's lootin' and plunderin' and raisin' all kinds of hell between the Sawtooths and Texas. And there's nothin' to stop him but a few women, some scrawny kids, and maybe a few stove-up old-timers like myself."

"You don't look so stove-up."

"I ain't showed you my scars," Charlie said, a sudden gleam in his eye. "But I got 'em. I can still lick a man half my age."

"You know where I can find this Hawk Fletcher."

"Ain't no trick to that. He lives in Hell Town."

"So I heard. Whereabouts is that? The Sawtooth's a big range."

"I could take you there. If I had a mind to."

"Now, why would you want to do a thing like that?"

"You got your reasons, I got mine." Charlie finished his coffee and tossed the dregs onto the fire. Then he put down the cup and relit his pipe, his face thoughtful, his gray eyes brooding.

"I'm listening," prompted Fargo.

"About five years ago, I made the only honest-to-God strike of my career. I had a pretty little Mexican spitfire with me then, and she sure as hell knew how to comfort a man's couch. She was also a hell of a worker; did what I said when I said and helped me pan about two thousand in gold dust from this here stream I found."

Fargo took out his cigar and relit it.

"We was getting ready to move on, the gold already packed away in leather pouches inside the aparejos on

23

my mules when this fellow Hank Fletcher rode into camp. That's right. He was just Hank Fletcher then. But he was tall enough and had a look about him that excited my woman." Charlie took the stem out of his mouth and spat. "That night she took off with him, and took all my gold with her."

Fargo raised his eyebrows in surprise, but said nothing. He understood perfectly now why the old prospector would welcome a chance to get even.

"Wouldn't a been so bad if she'd just taken the share belonged to her," Charlie said, musing. "She always knew it was hers whenever she wanted to pull out."

"You made that clear to her?"

"I did."

"Maybe that was your mistake."

"I done figured that out, too." Charlie looked squarely at Fargo. "So now you see why I wouldn't mind makin' that trip to Hell Town with you."

"What can you tell me about the place?"

"It's just a town hidden away in the Sawtooths—and with enough hostiles in the mountains to keep away most people. They got all they need there. Women and warehouses to keep their goods. It's where the Comanches come to trade, and any other Indians willin' to make the trip."

"How many men has Hawk Fletcher got riding for him?"

"Hard to say. Maybe fifty or seventy-five, not countin' families and hangers-on. Close to a hundred and fifty including them. Could be a lot more than that now. The pickin's has been mighty good these past months."

Fargo recalled the sight of Hawk and his band driving Conchita's stock and belongings before them as they galloped off. Yes. The pickings had been pretty damn good on that particular day, and they would undoubtedly get a whole lot better in the months ahead.

"Just tell me the quickest route to their place," Fargo requested. "That's all I need."

"You goin' to march in there all by your lonesome and call out Hawk Fletcher to a personal duel? That it?"

"Hell, no."

"Then you need help. That's an army he's got, an' every man in that army kills as easy as a dog bites fleas. You can't do it alone. An' if you try, that woman you told me about ain't goin' to get her vengeance."

"So you want to throw in with me? You think that would even the odds, do you?"

"Be a start," Charlie said, spitting into the fire.

Fargo found that impossible to dispute, but he didn't see how it changed anything. He puffed on his cigar and leaned back, enjoying it.

"We got visitors," Charlie told him conversationally, tapping the tobacco out of his clay pipe. "Just sit right where you are, and whatever you do, don't make no sudden moves."

Charlie stood up casually. Carrying his empty cup with him, he walked over to the wagon. Fargo heard the tailgate slam down and then the squeak of the wagon's springs as Kettle stepped up into it. As if he didn't have a care in the world, the old-timer began to whistle tunelessly. Puffing idly on his cigar, Fargo let his hand drop casually to the Colt resting in his holster.

The first attack came from directly across the narrow stream. One of the four Kiowas they had discouraged earlier rose suddenly from a bed of reeds and raced toward him through the shallow water, his lance held high over his shoulder. As the brave let fly with his lance, Fargo drew his Colt and flung himself off the log. The blade of the lance buried itself in the wood, the haft quivering with the impact.

The brave let out his battle cry and brandished his hatchet, his painted face distorted. Fargo steadied his Colt on a boulder embedded in the sand and squeezed the trigger. The Indian's face disintegrated, yet the crazed warrior kept on coming, his legs striding mechanically. As he left the water and struck the soft sand, the hatchet dropped from his nerveless fingers and his feet melted from under him.

Firing erupted behind Fargo. Flinging himself over, he saw an Indian staggering back from the rear of the wagon. Then Charlie Kettle thrust his head and shoulders out through the opening, a huge Walker Colt in his hand. He looked in Fargo's direction, aimed, and pulled the trigger.

The slug slammed loudly into someone behind Fargo. Hearing the impact, Fargo twisted around and saw that the bullet had slammed directly into an onrushing Kiowa's naked chest. Fargo ducked aside, but not fast enough to get out of the way of the dying Kiowa's plunging body. As the Indian slammed into him, he heard Charlie fire again. Another brave staggered, then slammed facedown into the still-smoldering campfire. As the Indian's head struck the fire, the coffeepot went clattering away.

His gun still smoking, Charlie Kettle walked over and looked down at Fargo. "You got blood all over your shirt," he told him. "You ain't hit, are you?"

Fargo pushed the dead Indian off him and got to his feet. "No, I'm all right," he replied, peeling off the shirt and dropping it into the stream. "Thanks to you."

"Looks like we both got reason to thank the other," Charlie said, glancing around him at the sprawled bodies.

Fargo walked into the stream and scrubbed most of the blood off his shirt, then wrung it out. As he dropped the shirt over his head and shoulders, he glanced over at Charlie Kettle.

"You knew those Kiowa had sneaked back. I didn't. How the hell did you manage that?"

"I was expectin' them. They been tailin' me for a couple days now. I knew they was doin' it, but they didn't know I did."

"So you figured they'd be returning, and kept your eye peeled," Fargo said, breaking open his Colt so he could reload it.

Charlie nodded agreeably. "That's about it. That savage across the stream was a mite careless. When he was moving through the reeds, the sun glinted off the tip of his lance."

Fargo nodded, then frowned, as a change in the wind's direction brought the smell of singed flesh to him. Charlie caught the stench, too, and walked over and dragged the Indian out of the campfire's embers, after which he recovered the coffeepot and rinsed it out in the stream.

"We better be movin' on," Charlie said, standing up with the clean pot in his hands. "This here campsite is beginnin' to stink some."

Fargo nodded. He didn't have to say anything. He knew what Charlie Kettle was thinking. In the last few minutes, the old-timer had convinced the Trailsman that it wouldn't hurt any to let him join Fargo in his search for Hawk Fletcher.

"Yeah," said Fargo, dropping his reloaded Colt back into his holster. "You're right. We better get movin'."

3

Riding alongside the wagon, Fargo pulled up. Charlie
yelled at his two mules and yanked hopefully back on
the reins. Somewhere in the wagon a metal pan
clanged.

Bent Rock, the town they were heading for, was in
sight. They gazed at the low collection of buildings in
the distance for a few moments, drinking in the sight,
then started up again. They had left west Texas and
were in Arizona Territory, the bleak Sawtooth range
looming in the distance—as far away today, it seemed,
as it had looked for the past three days.

As they approached the town about a half hour
later, its main elements became clearer. The pitiless
Arizona sun had twisted and bleached the unpainted
sidings of many of the buildings, while others
had been neatly whitewashed. Close by the creek
on the other side of town, Fargo glimpsed a scattering

of neat adobe houses set upon narrow streets. From their midst loomed a church steeple.

As they rode into the town, the air rang with the clang of the smithy's hammer and the shouts of men hailing each other. Pulling up in front of the livery stable, Fargo dismounted and led his pinto inside. Charlie followed a few moments later with his un-hitched mules.

The hostler told Charlie he could leave his wagon out front for now, but reminded him to park it behind the livery barn before night fell. Charlie agreed amia-bly enough; then he and Fargo crossed the street to the hotel and registered. A visit to the barbershop fol-lowed, after which they found a restaurant in the Spanish section, fronting a gleaming, well-swept plaza. They ate at tables set out under awnings. The meal was hot enough for them both, and they leaned back finally, sipping beer contentedly as the brilliant sky lost its glow.

The church impressed Fargo.

"You mind explaining this town to me?" Fargo asked Charlie. "What keeps it alive out here?"

Charlie pointed to the hills looming more darkly now at sunset. "Silver. Plenty of it. There must be close to twelve silver mines up in there. This town feeds on them."

"And Hawk Fletcher leaves this town alone?"

"For a price."

"What's that?"

"Let's put it this way. When he drops in or stays here for any length of time, he likes not being noticed. And I heard once that he has a woman here."

"You think that's true?"

Charlie shrugged. "It's just a rumor. I heard it two, maybe three years ago."

"Maybe we'd better drift around, ask a few questions."

Charlie looked at him. "We won't have to ask a thing."

"What do you mean?"

"I'm figurin' Hawk's men are all around—looking out for strangers like us, strangers who might be askin' too many questions."

"I guess that makes sense, all right."

"So what's our next move?" Charlie asked.

"I still think I'll do some prowling. If I do meet any of Hawk Fletcher's gunsels, maybe I could make noises like I wanted to join up with him. Hell, they might even be looking for recruits."

"That's a dangerous game to play."

"But I won't be playing it alone, will I?"

Charlie grinned. "Guess maybe I could keep an eye on you, at that."

"I'll be counting on it." Fargo stood up. "I'll move out first. Give me room, Charlie. Don't hang too close."

Charlie downed his beer. "Don't you worry none about that. I'll move my wagon in behind the livery first, then follow after you."

Fargo nodded and moved off.

The Hanging Man Saloon was crammed with dedicated gamblers and equally dedicated drinking men, with almost as many Mexican bar girls. Fargo pushed himself through the batwings, probed carefully past the poker and faro tables, and eventually found himself near enough to the bar to be able to push himself through the crush and gain the attention of the barkeep. Purchasing a bottle of bourbon, he hauled it and a shot glass over to a table along one wall, then collapsed gratefully into one of its two chairs.

About a quarter of an hour later, out of the corner of his eye, he saw Charlie entering, but gave no indication that he saw or knew him. Lifting his bottle to pour himself another drink, he caught sight of a Mexican approaching.

The Mexican had almost reached his table before Fargo realized the Mexican was a woman. She wore a man's hat, bandanna, shirt, and Levi's. Spurs chinked on her boots as she neared him, and if it had not been for the glowing health of her dark complexion and the unmistakable swell under her checked shirt, he would not have known.

Halting before his table, she took off her hat. Black curls cascaded down onto her shoulders. In that instant she became all woman. "Mind if I join you?" she asked.

Fargo shrugged.

She sat down. "My name's Rita. I work here. Sometimes. I'm off tonight."

"Can't get enough of the place, huh?"

She shrugged.

"My name's Skye—Skye Fargo."

"You are new in town," she said. "I saw you ride in."

Fargo looked more closely at her and nodded.

"You come far?"

"Far enough."

She laughed and waved over another girl, who appeared quickly, carrying a bottle of wine and a glass for her. "You sure you don't mind if I drink with you?"

"I appreciate the company," Fargo told her.

Nodding, Rita poured herself a drink. "I think maybe you don't know about this place."

"What is that supposed to mean?"

"Bent Rock is dangerous for strangers. Have you come for the silver mines?"

"Nope."

She smiled brilliantly, the clean white of her teeth flashing in her dusky face. "You do not say much, Skye."

"Never found an open mouth to accomplish much," he drawled, pouring himself a drink.

"You are a very wise man," she told him.

"Why'd you stop at my table, Rita?"

"To warn you."

"To get out of Bent Rock?"

"Yes—unless you have good reason to be here."

"As a matter of fact, there is a place I would rather be. A place called Hell Town."

She frowned, then gazed at him for a moment, shrewdly. "I think maybe I hear of such a place."

He smiled. "I had an idea you might've."

She tipped her head. "Why do you want to find Hell Town? It is deep in the mountains, many miles from here."

"There's a fellow I'm looking for. Figure I should

be able to find him there. Hawk Fletcher. Maybe I'd like to join up with him."

"Maybe?"

"That's what I said," Fargo said.

"You know this Fletcher?"

"Let's say I met him once."

"Where?" Rita asked.

"In Texas."

"You . . . ride with him?"

Fargo knew how important his next response would be. He decided to take a chance. "Sure," he said. "For a while."

She straightened slightly and poured herself another glass of wine. Sipping it, she leaned back in her chair and regarded him coldly. After a while she said, "I think maybe I can help you."

"I was hoping you could."

"But first we become friends."

Fargo's eyebrows went up a notch. "That suits me fine," he admitted easily.

She nodded briskly. "Good. You come to my place tonight."

"Come to you where?"

"You know the church?"

Fargo nodded.

"The third adobe hut down, toward river. You cannot miss it. I will put lantern in window. The lantern will have blue chimney."

"Not red."

"No," she responded easily, smiling. "Not red."

She stood up then, took her bottle and glass back to the bar, paid up, and strode from the saloon. As she disappeared through the batwings, Fargo saw quite a few pair of eyes swing in his direction and more than a few knowing smiles.

One of the men who had turned to look at him, a burly Mexican, caught Fargo's eyes and raised his glass in a salute to him. "*Bueno*," he cried. "That one, she sleep with only the best bulls in corral."

A roar of laughter greeted that assertion. Fargo refilled his glass, held it up in salute to the packed saloon, then tossed it down.

A moment later, he followed Rita from the saloon.

The blue lantern was glowing softly in the window, as Rita had told him it would. He knocked softly on the door. It opened immediately and he was pulled urgently inside. She was wearing nothing, and in the light from the lantern her naked body glowed an almost unearthly blue, intensifying the darkness of her pubic hair.

"Undress," she hissed, drawing him into her bedroom.

As he pulled off his boots, her hands worked swiftly to unbutton his buckskin shirt and then the fly to his pants. His gun belt and knife sheath she hung up on a peg behind the bedroom door; his clothes she draped over a wooden chair.

Then she pulled him eagerly down onto her.

As they embraced, she whispered huskily in his ear, "I see you go to barbershop after you ride in, and I know you one big man. That is what I like. Big men who are clean."

"You ain't so bad yourself."

"I will show you!"

Her hand slid down between them and grasped him firmly. The electric touch of her hand on his hot, turgid shaft sent desire surging through his groin. He moved up onto her, positioning himself for the plunge. Laughing softly, she helped him find her entrance, and he rammed his shaft deep into her hot, moist depths. She dug her fingernails into his back and, lifting her legs, pressed her heels against the back of his legs.

"You not need much preparation this time," she told him, her hot breath bathing his ear.

"What about you?"

"Do not apologize. When I see you in saloon, I begin to get moist. Until you knock on my door, I think my knees turn to water. I am ready now. Say no more. Move! Take me!"

She moved her hips from side to side, then surged upward, the enveloping warmth of her closing like a fist about his shaft. He almost gasped out loud. Seizing her hips, he began plunging recklessly down into her, hitting bottom with each stroke.

"Slowly," she cried hoarsely. "We have the night."

He pulled back quickly and nodded, grinning down at her. Her cheeks were flushed, her features tense, her nostrils flaring. Keeping himself under rigid control, he resumed his steady, metronomic thrusting, only gradually increasing the tempo and doing so in time to her own building excitement. Soon her hips increased their smooth, maddening gyrations, and before long, she began slamming up at him even more fiercely than before, her movements timed perfectly with his.

He leaned forward and kissed her, his lips opening hers hungrily as he sucked on her full lower lip. With his tongue he probed hungrily into her mouth as she writhed in ecstasy under him. Then she flung her arms around his back and squeezed, uttering tiny little cries. It was a headlong race by then, all controls off. She began hissing at him in Spanish while she tossed her head from side to side, her dark penumbra of hair exploding across her pillow.

Caught up fully himself by now, he abandoned himself to his frenzy and met her thrust for thrust, driving himself into her with a violence that surprised him as the sudden, inevitable rush of ecstasy overtook him.

"No," she cried. "Do not stop now! Keep going!"

But she need not have worried. He had no intention of stopping. Hell, there was no way he could! Out of control now—and yet marvelously in control—he piled into her, stroking with an intensity he was almost afraid would injure her.

At last she was over the top. Bucking with a sudden, shuddering force, she flung her head back. A tight scream broke from her throat while he, still driving furiously, went careening wildly over the edge after her.

He lay on his side watching her as the heavy pounding of his heart subsided and his breathing returned to normal. The quilt moved up and down over the curves of her breasts as she breathed. Her hair was scattered across her face. Brushing it back, she met his gaze, then smiled and reached back to the night table and produced a couple of cheroots.

Handing him one, she took the other one for herself. A match flared. She lit hers, then his, after which she scooted up so her back was resting against the headboard. As she did so, the blanket fell away from her, revealing her large, firm, melonlike breasts and her slender back from her shoulders to her hips. She inhaled deeply on the cheroot and tossed her head to slip her hair back.

He put his hand on one breast, cupped it for a moment or two, then let his hand glide down her silken skin to her hipbone. She smiled at him and opened her thighs slightly. He rested his hand for a moment in the hot, moist warmth of her, then moved his hand back up to her breast and cupped it again in his rough hand, feeling her large nipple with his fingers. She smiled at him, enjoying his exploration, encouraging him.

"Why does a girl like you go around in men's clothes?" he asked.

"They are more comfortable," she responded easily. "It is not possible to ride properly sidesaddle. Besides, with a dress or skirt, riding astride is an embarrassment."

He nodded, his hand still cupping her breast.

"This man, Hawk Fletcher," she said. Without disturbing his hand, she pulled the blanket up over her nakedness, her eyes appraising now, careful. "You like him?"

"He knows what he wants."

38

"That is important?"

"If you want to get something done right," Fargo said.

"Fletcher and his riders have killed many people, innocent people. Is this not so? And often he ride with the Comanche. You like that?"

Fargo shrugged. "Fletcher shares his booty equally with his men. And they live well. They have their women with them and all they can eat and drink. Yes, I think I would like that."

"You are right, I suppose," she admitted. "His men live well, and they have country of their own, deep in the Sawtooths. There they are safe; no one can find them."

"That's what I hear."

"It is strange," she said.

"What's strange?"

"When I make love to man I find out what kind of man he is. A pig in the saddle is a pig in bed. A man with no character, he do not try to please a woman, only himself. A man ruthless enough to kill the inno-cents, he is not one who smile when he make love . . . as you do."

"You mean I don't pass the test."

"I mean you confuse me."

"Maybe this time, that test of yours is no good."

"That is true. You are big man, powerful. You have lake-blue eyes, but they can be as cold as ice. I see that in saloon. Your gun belt has seen many years, and your Colt is well-oiled. And you are drifter who once ride with Hawk Fletcher in Texas."

"Confused?"

She shrugged and stubbed her cheroot out on a saucer on the night table. "Yes. But it does not matter."

She took his hand away from her breast, flung aside the blanket, and stepped from the bed. At the same moment, the bedroom door was flung open and a tall, lean Mexican entered the room, a six-gun in his right hand, his dark eyes gleaming with malice. Fargo jumped to his feet.

"This man want to rejoin Fletcher," Rita told the newcomer, her voice laced with contempt. "He ride with him in Texas."

"You dirty, son of a bitch," the Mexican said, advancing on Fargo, then raising the six-gun over his head.

Fargo flung up his right forearm as the Mexican brought the six-gun down hard. Glancing off his forearm, the gun barrel managed to crunch down on the side of Fargo's head. Fargo staggered back, aware that his attacker was unwilling to shoot him, since the sound of gunfire on such a quiet night would bring a crowd.

Reaching back to the wall to steady himself, Fargo held up his left hand.

"Hold it," he cried. "You're making a mistake."

"No we not, you gringo bastard," the Mexican snarled. "Now you take us to Fletcher, or we kill you!"

"Hell! I don't know where the son of a bitch is!"

"You lie!" cried Rita.

Where the hell was Charlie Kettle? Fargo asked himself as he braced himself against the wall, then launched himself suddenly at the Mexican. The fellow tried to club Fargo a second time, but his gun barrel only glanced off the back of Fargo's head as Fargo swept in under the gun and slammed his head and shoulders into the man's midsection.

With some astonishment, Fargo felt the Mexican's body jackknife easily, startled at how light and insubstantial the man was. Driving him back fiercely, Fargo slammed him brutally against the opposite wall. So hard did the Mexican strike it he dropped his weapon and hung limply against the wall. Fargo cuffed him in the face, then buried a left and then a right into the man's midsection. He felt as if he were punching through a scarecrow. He saw the Mexican's face go green, all fight drained out of him. Stepping back, Fargo let the man sag painfully to the floor. As soon as he hit it, the Mexican bent over, retching dryly, then passed out.

Fargo turned to search the floor for the Colt the Mexican had dropped. But Rita had already snatched it up. Backing away from Fargo, she leveled it at his midsection and thumb-cocked it, her gun hand trembling slightly.

"Just let me explain," said Fargo. "You've made a mistake about me. Just give me a chance to explain."

"I give you no chance to explain. I kill you!"

"Hold it right there, lady."

The sharp command came from the open doorway. Startled, the woman swung her gun in that direction. Charlie Kettle was standing in the doorway with a six-gun trained on her. She could have fired then, but she hesitated. In that instant, Fargo leapt at her. Grabbing the gun barrel, he twisted it brutally out of her hand.

She fell back upon the bed, holding her right hand, tears of rage coursing down her cheeks.

Fargo glanced over at Charlie and grinned. "What kept you?"

"Hell, you told me to give you plenty of room."

Fargo chuckled. "Not *that* much room."

"Mind tellin' me what's goin' on here?" Charlie asked, stepping into the bedroom and grinning at Fargo's pale, gaunt nakedness. "Besides the obvious, I mean."

Fargo bent to pull on his britches and at the same time flung a blanket over Rita's naked shoulders. She was still bowed over, crying softly. Behind Fargo, the tall Mexican groaned softly.

"I wish I knew for sure," Fargo told Charlie. "At first I thought Rita here was going to help me join up with Hawk Fletcher. Then this buddy of hers walked in with a Colt."

"Why?"

"The way I figure it, because they believed I'd once ridden with Hawk Fletcher."

"You mean they ain't on Fletcher's side?"

"It don't look that way."

Charlie walked closer to Rita. She was still weeping softly. "Miss," he said gently, "you got us wrong. Fargo and me, we're on your side. We hate that son of a bitch Fletcher as much as you do."

She looked up at him, her eyes narrowed in suspicion. "You expect me to believe that?"

"He's telling the truth," said Fargo, stepping closer and smiling down at Rita. "I told you I rode with him once and wanted to join up with him again so maybe you'd help me find the bastard. But we want him for the same reason you do."

"That's right," Charlie said cheerfully. "We'd like to see him hang."

Now Rita was angry. "But why did you not say so before this?"

"I wasn't sure what you were up to or what side you were on. We figure there's more than a few of Fletcher's men in this town, keeping an eye out."

"That is true," she admitted, brushing back her hair and wrapping the blanket about her more tightly. She took a deep sigh, then looked in some relief from Fargo to Charlie. "Yes, in this town you do have to be careful."

She left the bed then and moved past Fargo to kneel beside the still-groggy Mexican Fargo had cut down. Looking back up at Fargo, she said, "This is my brother, Pedro Mendoza. He is very weak because of what this animal Fletcher do to him."

"What was that?"

"Later I tell you. Now help me lift him onto my bed."

Fargo bent and lifted the barely conscious Mexican off the floor, again aware of how light he was. Placing him down gently on the bed, he stepped back while Rita pulled off his boots, unbuttoned his shirt, then pulled the blanket up over him.

His eyes flickered open. He seemed about to say something, but Rita put a finger to her lips.

"Rest," she whispered to him softly. "It is all right now." Then she turned to Fargo and Charlie. "Go into the kitchen and wait for me. I have some tequila. I think maybe we all need it."

They went into her kitchen and sat down at the table. A moment later Rita appeared in a long robe. Tying the sash about her waist, she walked to the cupboards over the sink, lifted a jug of tequila down from a shelf, filled three large mugs and brought them over to them. Then she sat down at the table across from them. In wry salute, they raised their glasses and drank heartily of the fiery liquor.

"Now," said Fargo, "tell us what happened."

"There is not so much to tell. Six months ago, Fletcher and his Comancheros attack our *estancia* on the border. Both my parents he kill. He take our horses and burn our hacienda, and Pedro, he was hurt so bad, he still is not strong. He take bullet in his gut."

"Ouch," said Charlie softly. "He's lucky to be alive."

"We live for only one thing now; to bring this pig Fletcher down, to trample him in the dust."

"How would killing me have helped?"

"We not going to kill you. Take you prisoner."

"Why?"

"If you ride before with Fletcher, like you tell me, maybe you know how to find him again. So I make love to you, and once you have no clothes and your gun is hung up on peg, we make you our prisoner so you have to take us to Fletcher."

"That was your plan, eh?"

"Yes."

"Sorry, Rita. Like I said in there, I never rode with

44

that bastard. And I got my own reasons for finding him."

"Why you lie to me in saloon?"

"I figured you might be one of Fletcher's people, on the lookout for new recruits."

"So you see," said Charlie, "we're just as much in the dark as you are. All we know for certain is that Hawk Fletcher's place is hidden somewhere in the Sawtooths. Trouble is, that range is more'n a couple hundred miles square, most of it vertical."

Rita frowned. "Not so long ago we trail wagons through pass we think go to Hell Town," she said. "The wagons have new girls for his men. But Pedro get very weak and we have to come back here."

Fargo glanced shrewdly at Charlie. "We could pick up the trail left by those wagons," he said.

"I do not think so," Rita said. "The wagons are gone many days now."

"How long?"

"Six, maybe seven days."

"It hasn't rained, has it?" the Trailsman asked.

"No rain for many weeks."

Fargo looked at Charlie. "I say we take a chance. If it's a route his men take often enough, we should have no trouble finding it. It should be a well-worn trail by now. If it's not, it'll still point us in the right direction." Fargo turned to Rita. "Tomorrow, will you show us the pass they headed for?"

Rita looked from Fargo to Charlie, her eyes brightening. "Yes. I can do that."

"Thanks."

"You go into mountains? You follow the wagons?"

"I don't think we have any other choice," said Fargo.

"Then maybe you take Pedro and me."

"Now wait a minute."

"You cannot go without us. We help. I cook for you."

"Trackin' an animal like that, it's better we travel light," Charlie explained. "The fewer the better."

Fargo nodded his agreement and stood up. He realized suddenly that he had to get dressed and that he was suddenly very, very tired.

"Sorry, Rita," he told her. "You just leave that bastard to us. We'll take care of him for you."

"I wish you change your mind."

"No chance of that," Charlie said.

As Fargo started back into Rita's bedroom for his clothes and gun belt, Rita pulled the jug of tequila closer and poured herself another drink. She seemed resigned and unhappy.

And determined to get herself good and drunk.

4

It was a sullen Rita Mendoza who rode with them as far as the pass that next morning. When Fargo tried to thank her, she wheeled her mount without a word and galloped back down the trail, disappearing finally in a cloud of alkaline dust.

Charlie looked up at Fargo from his wagon seat, a crooked smile on his bewhiskered face. "By grannies, I don't know as I like that," he said. "Hell hath no fury like a woman scorned, and that's the God's truth."

"Never mind. We got a long hot climb ahead of us, and I'm just as glad we ain't got her to contend with. That brother of hers is the nearest thing to a living dead man I ever saw."

"But you got to admit. He's got sand."

"I don't deny that," Fargo said, spurring his pinto ahead of the wagon. He was upset with himself and with Rita. He understood her desire to go with them, and admired her for it. They had argued fiercely that morning, and he had been forced to say some cruel things, such as the fact that she and her brother would be practically worthless if they came upon trouble of any kind, especially Comanches or Kiowas. As he tried to point out to her, sentiment counted for little at a time like this.

Fargo was certain he had done the right thing. After all, what he and Charlie were contemplating was stopping a ruthless marauder and his entire band, a task about as easy to accomplish as taking fresh meat from a grizzly. There was no sense in them two getting hurt any worse than they already were.

This was the clincher he had used on Rita. It should have consoled him, but it didn't.

Close to sundown they still hadn't reached the pass. As they emerged from a stand of pine, they saw a war party of about a dozen mounted Comanches riding up the gentle rise toward them. The Indians rode bareback, guiding their ponies with a single jaw rein, their ponies' tails tied up.

Fargo yanked the pinto to a halt. He heard Charlie curse beside him but did not look in his direction.

The Indians made no sound as they came on at a steady lope, carrying bows, war shields, and lances from which scalps fluttered like pennants. About half of them had rifles—ungainly flintlocks, their stocks gaudy with brass tacks hammered in. Their faces and bodies were covered with stripes of white, red, and yellow, each stripe accented with heavy strokes of black. All they wore were breechclouts and moccasins, the more showy boasting buggalo-horn or bear-claw headdresses. All of them were young warriors, Fargo realized, braves who had not tallied enough coups yet to warrant feathered bonnets.

The lead Comanche let out a high, keening war cry and waved the others on after him.

Fargo slipped quickly from his saddle. "Throw the mules if you can," he told Charlie.

Charlie had already leapt from his seat and was busy unhitching the two animals. Both animals were close to panic, having already caught the Indians' scent. Fargo snubbed the pinto's muzzle back close to the horn, picked up the off fetlock, and threw the Ovaro heavily. The startled pony began to kick his hind legs. Fargo caught one hind foot, then the other, and pig-tied them across the fore cannons.

Taking out his Sharps, he checked its load, then made sure he had enough linen cartridges in his side pocket. When the Indians started circling and it got pretty hot, he wouldn't have time for reloading, he knew. When that time came, he would have to rely on his Colt. But at a distance, a Sharps could sure as hell discourage a redskin. Fargo settled the barrel across his pony's neck and sighted carefully on the lead Comanche.

He squeezed the trigger, the sudden loud crack it made slamming back at him from the tree-mantled slopes around him. The lead rider's pony changed direction suddenly and ran wild as its rider slipped off into the grass.

"Nice shootin', Fargo," Charlie cried.

The prospector was behind the wagon, his mules lined up behind him. He wasn't going to try to throw

49

them. He had a Hawken in his hand, his huge Walker Colt on the wagon seat beside him. Aiming the Hawken carefully, he squeezed off a shot.

A Comanche lost his mount. The horse somersaulted, the Comanche springing clear, unhurt. The formation opened up then as the Indians bent low over their horses and came on hard. Fargo banged away at one off to his right. Unhurt, the Comanche dropped behind the pony, hanging by one heel and a loop of mane on its far side. Fargo saw the muzzle of the Comanche's rifle poking out from under his pony's neck—and sent a quick round at the mount.

It went down suddenly and the Indian landed on his feet and raced back to get out of range. Charlie brought him down with his Hawken. At that, the remaining Comanches, now at full gallop, let loose with a series of war cries that caused the hair to stand up on the back of Fargo's neck. He shook off the fear and reloaded, aware that it was no real shame to be so affected by an Indian's war cry. Unless he was already dead, there was no white man living who could remain unaffected by it.

Lifting his Sharps, Fargo tracked the nearest Comanche, but even as he squeezed the trigger, the Indians broke into a circle. His shot went wild. Fargo put aside his Sharps and grabbed his Colt. The Comanches were within twenty or thirty yards now as they swept around the two of them, firing from under their horses' necks and tails with both rifles and bows.

The air was suddenly lethal with missiles. Bullets buzzed over, whispering death; others exploded in the ground in front of him. Beside Fargo, the contents of the wagon were getting a beating as the Comanches' bullets slapped through the canvas and rattled among the pots and pans and the rest of Charlie's mining equipment.

Through all this, the pinto was wild-eyed, terrified, and made futile efforts to right himself, despite Fargo's efforts to calm it. A mule screamed and went down behind Charlie, who almost left the cover of his wagon to overtake the savage responsible. Fargo heard Charlie's huge Walker banging away in concert with his Colt and saw two more Comanches tumble off their ponies. An unhorsed Comanche raced screaming toward Fargo. His right foot came down solidly on a boulder embedded in the earth, and from it he launched himself through the air. Fargo hit him while he was still airborne. He landed less than a foot in front of the pinto, his brains blown out.

The Comanches pulled back. As they went, Fargo counted only seven left. He felt pretty damn good about that. The two of them had accounted for almost half the war party.

Pulling up out of range, the Comanches seemed to be jabbering at one another with considerable energy.

Fargo checked his supply of ammunition, then glanced over at Charlie. "How's your ammunition?"

"I got enough for one more charge. But that's all."

"Same here."

The Comanches regrouped and came hard once again. After all, they must have told one another, there were only two white men—and *they* were the Comanche, the Terror of the Plains.

Fargo had reloaded his Sharps and between his lips he held a linen cartridge. He aimed more carefully this time as the war party came on, tracking a big, broad-chested son of a bitch wearing a pair of buffalo horns, and squeezed off his shot. The round slammed into the brave's chest like a fist and he went ass over teakettle off the pony's hind end. This should have discouraged the other Comanches, but it didn't.

They went into their famous Comanche wheel once more and Fargo's Sharps blew a hole in the side of another Comanche. But they came on just as enthusiastically, at times drifting in as close as ten feet, filling the air with arrows and lead. Fargo lost his hat and felt a sudden, branding pain on the top of his right shoulder. Ignoring it, he lifted his Colt and pumped shot after shot at the ring of screaming savages.

Then one broke between Fargo and Charlie, leapt from his horse and onto the wagon tongue. Charlie jumped up beside him and swiped him across the chops with the barrel of his Hawken. The Comanche went flying, landed on his back, then ran off, holding his head with both hands. Another Comanche yanked his pony out of the circle and headed for Fargo. Fargo ducked down behind the pinto and fired up at the belly of the Comanche's pony as he sailed over him. His shot reamed the pony's gut, and the pony went sprawling. The Comanche landed on his feet and headed back for Fargo, screaming at the top of his lungs.

A shot rang out from the pines above them. The slug caught the Comanche in the back and sent him sprawling facedown. Again a shot came from the same spot, and another Comanche went flying off his pony. Then a fusilade of rifle and handgun fire rained down upon the startled Comanches. Dismayed, they swerved away from Fargo and Charlie, breaking their circle. In utter confusion the remaining Comanches began firing frantically at whoever it was in the pines.

Taking advantage of their confusion, Fargo flung up his Sharps, loaded, and tracked the biggest and loudest of the Comanches, blasted him off his pony. That did it. The few remaining Comanches wheeled their ponies and galloped back and out of range, pulling up in some confusion.

"Who the hell's in the pines?" Fargo asked Charlie.

"Don't ask no questions," replied Charlie. "Just be grateful."

Fargo nodded and studied the parleying Comanches.

A moment later the Indians, no longer screaming, and riding upright on their ponies trotted back toward them.

"Leave them be," said Fargo. "They're coming for their dead."

Fargo watched as the Comanches picked up their dismounted and their dead, then wheeled and galloped off. A moment later they had vanished back into the pines from which they had emerged.

Fargo loosed the pigging string and got the pinto back onto his feet. The animal was trembling from head to tail, his flanks rippling like water. Patting his neck steadily, Fargo calmed him, mounted up, and turned the pony toward the pines above them.

"I'll ride up there and see who it was lent a hand," Fargo told Charlie.

"Never mind," said Charlie. "Look."

Fargo glanced back and saw two riders break out of the timber. One of them was Rita and the other was her brother, Pedro. Both had broad smiles on their faces.

Fargo sighed. He was going to have to eat crow, he realized. But what the hell.

Pulling up beside the wagon, Rita and her brother dismounted, their faces showing not triumph now, only concern. "We heard the firing and rode hard to get here," Rita said, her face flushed.

"And we're right glad you did," Charlie told her.

"That's right," Fargo admitted, dismounting. "You saved our bacon, looks like."

"Seems to me you do okay without us," said Pedro, looking around at the dead horses littering the slope. "I think maybe these Comanche remember this battle long time."

"Well, *I* sure as hell will," said Charlie. "They killed one of my mules."

"Is that the extent of the damage?" Fargo asked.

"Yep." Then, peering at Fargo, the old man's eyes narrowed. "Hey, what happened to your shoulder?"

Fargo's left hand reached up and felt it. It came away bloody. Rita uttered a tiny cry of concern and stepped closer to examine the wound.

"It's only a flesh wound," said Fargo. "I hardly felt it."

"You was just too busy to notice," Charlie told him. "I knowed a feller had his leg shot off during a misun-

54

derstanding with some Apaches. He didn't notice it until he tried to step into his stirrup."

"You have lost much blood," said Rita. She was frowning anxiously as her fingers poked through the tear in his shirt. "You will soon feel very weak if we do not stop the flow."

Fargo realized then that he did feel a bit woozy. He took a step toward the wagon and his knees almost buckled. Charlie stepped close and helped him into the wagon. As Rita climbed in after him and tried to clear a place for him to lie down, Fargo felt the universe begin to spin crazily.

He started to say something, and passed out.

A couple of days later they were camped some miles beyond the pass. It was night and the sky overhead was alive with stars, set like jewels on a velvet cloth. Pedro was standing guard, and Charlie was snoring away under the wagon. Rita had left her soogan and come over to see how he was feeling. Now the two sat side by side, each smoking a cheroot, Rita with her back against a boulder, Fargo sitting against a tree trunk.

Fargo turned his head to glance up at Pedro's distant figure outlined on a ridge. Somewhere a coyote yipped. He looked back at Rita. "Your brother seems a lot stronger these past couple of days."

Rita smiled, her teeth bright in her dusky face. "You see? This travel is good for him. It give him heart to know we will soon find this cockroach Fletcher. It is all he live for."

"And you?"

"I too think of nothing else."

"It's not going to be easy, you know."

"When I see Fletcher, it will be easy," she said, her voice cold and deadly. "You will see."

Fargo said nothing for a while, content to puff on his smoke. His shoulder wound was not entirely healed, but he was able now to move it without wincing. A few hours before sunset, he had even brought down a jackrabbit with his Colt, using his right hand. He realized he owed much of the speed of his recovery to Rita, and was grateful.

He glanced at her. "I been wondering."

"Yes?"

"That time we had in bed back there—at your place in Bent Rock. That wasn't all faked."

She laughed huskily and tipped her head back against the boulder. "At first, it was," she admitted. "But then my body, it take over. Then all I wanted was you. I could not fake that."

He chuckled. "That's for sure."

"You not get no ideas now," she warned him quickly. "You still sick man, don' forget."

"You saw me track that rabbit and bring it down."

"I am no rabbit."

"No, but I got something here might bring you down." He glanced at the tent that had grown under his blanket just over his crotch.

She laughed huskily. "I been noticing," she admitted.

He flicked away his cheroot. It bounced on some rocks below, showering sparks with each bounce. She

56

sighed and dug her cheroot's tip into the ground, then moved closer.

He flicked aside his blanket. Swiftly unpeeling her pants, Rita eased herself in under his blanket, her arms snaking up around his neck.

"I wait long time for this," she whispered. "This time it is not just my body wants you."

He kissed her hard. That was how he felt too.

Almost a week had passed since they left the pass behind, and the trace worn by the wagons leaving Bent Rock was still visible. Along with the tracks of heavily laden wagons, however, they noticed as well the tracks of countless unshod ponies. Comanches, no doubt. Doing business with Hawk Fletcher and his Comancheros.

They talked this over one morning before setting out. The Indian sign had been getting so heavy, they figured it was only blind luck that had enabled them to avoid hostiles thus far. It was then they decided to abandon the wagon tracks and keep in the timber, well above the trace.

A couple of days later, close to sundown, the four of them pulled up suddenly. A deep, steady pounding—as if the mountain under their feet had grown a human heart—had gradually filled the air about them. It was uncanny. It seemed as if their hearts were attempting to beat in time with the titanic throbbing.

They were just above the timberline, a high, boulder-strewn ridge loomed off to their right. There was nothing visible beyond it but the dim ragged outline of distant peaks. The heavy, thumping beat was coming from just beyond that ridge.

"No secret what that is," said Charlie, tying his reins around his brake handle and stepping down from his wagon seat. "A stamping mill."

Grabbing his Hawken, he headed for the ridge. Chuckling, Fargo realized the prospector was right. There must be a mine below them on the other side of that ridge. He and Rita and Pedro dismounted and followed after the prospector. Reaching the crest of the ridge, they peered around a massive boulder and caught sight of a mining operation that filled almost entirely a small, cramped valley far below.

"There it is," Charlie said, pointing the stamping mill out to them.

Fargo saw it clearly enough. Now that they were in sight of it, the steady, monotonous pounding seemed to come directly from it. Fargo saw, too, the many other plank-and-log buildings that had been constructed about the mine shaft and the spiderweb of trestles that led from the shaft to the ore chutes. Below the chutes, Fargo was able to pick out the high-sided ore wagons, huge workhorses stamping in their traces.

Fargo noted the great piles of slag that filled almost every available spot of cleared ground. Stables for the horses and living quarters and stores for the miners had been built some distance north of the mine shaft. Thick coils of wood smoke from the engines driving the stamping mill, the hoists, and the pumps hung low over the valley, obscuring the patches of pine still left on the slopes high above it. The lower slopes were almost completely denuded, pocked with tree stumps and ravaged with gulleys and landslides.

"It's a silver mine, I'm thinkin'," said Charlie. He pointed to a road leading north out of the valley. "I'd say that leads to Ouray in Colorado. They got smelters there that can handle silver as well as gold, an' there's talk of a railroad comin' in soon's they get over that unpleasantness back East."

"You think Hawk Fletcher is running this mine?"

"It's in his own backyard, ain't it? There's talk he has a lot more mines than just this one. He's a greedy son of a bitch, that one."

"Could we go down there?" Rita asked. "And buy some fresh provisions from the men running it?"

Charlie grinned at Fargo, like a possum eating yellow jackets. "Maybe that ain't such a bad idea. We do need provisions, at that. Only I'm not talkin' about buyin'."

Pedro laughed. "*Bueno*," he said. "So maybe we sneak down there tonight and take what we need. Hawk Fletcher wouldn't like that."

"Just what I was thinkin'," admitted Charlie.

Rita spoke up. "If we do go down there, maybe we go first around to the gorge on other side, near that stream?"

They followed her pointing finger. Spilling out of the mountainside north of the mill was a swift stream that had already sliced a deep gorge through the mountain's flank. The slopes on both sides of the stream were so steep and rough that timber still clothed its banks. Rita was right. The gorge offered excellent cover. Furthermore, it opened out onto the valley floor only a few hundred yards from the mine's general store and what appeared to be the miners' living quarters.

Charlie turned to Fargo. "What do you think, Fargo?"

Fargo had already made up his mind. Rita was right. They could sure use fresh provisions. "I say we move out soon's it gets dark," he replied. "We should reach the gorge before midnight."

There was no more discussion. The four turned and walked back to Charlie's wagon.

Before clambering up onto his wagon seat, Charlie slapped his remaining mule affectionately on the rump. Glancing over at Fargo, he pointed to the mule and grinned. "I figure he'll be grindin' on real oats come mornin'."

"Don't count your oats before they're hatched," Fargo warned, stepping into his saddle.

The terrain would give them some trouble, Fargo realized. And he wasn't all that sure that robbing this here mine was going to be such a painless exercise. In addition, what to do with Rita sat heavily on his mind. There was no doubt that she and her brother had the backbone for whatever it took. But he didn't want them to go down before Fletcher's men. They had already suffered enough at the hands of that bastard.

But then, who hadn't?

Fargo swung his pinto around and headed back down into the pines, looking for a trail that would take them around the valley to that gorge.

5

They did not attack the mine that night.

It took considerably longer than they had antic-ipated to reach the gorge. Not until dawn did they find a way down the steep-sided draw to the stream, and only then because Fargo had decided finally that Charlie would have to leave his wagon on the rim and ride into the gorge on his mule. It was the right deci-sion as it turned out, since the mule—evidently pleased to be free of his traces—proved a durable and surefooted mount for Charlie, capable of leading them all down through the treacherous gullies and washes to the bank of the stream.

They selected a campsite well back from the gorge entrance and slept fitfully through most of the follow-ing day. Close to sundown, the four of them moved into the rocks at the entrance to the gorge and settled down to study the mine's layout.

What Fargo and the others noticed at once were the chains on the ankles of the miners, and the fact that most of them were Indians. The few white men among them were a scabrous lot, close to starvation, by the looks of them. The mine resembled a poorly run prison colony. The only thing lacking was the striped pants and shirts on the chained laborers.

"The Indians are Utes," said Fargo.

"And the others?" Rita asked, her voice hushed.

"Just poor devils caught up in Hawk Fletcher's net," Fargo said. "Tell me, did he take any male prisoners when he attacked your *estancia*?"

"*Sí*. Five men along with the women."

The four of them looked back at the miners trudging across the ground between the mine shaft and what appeared to be their living quarters, a long, low ramshackle building built on a slope. A frail-looking cook shack had been built not far from the barracks. Wood smoke was rising from its stack.

"Looks like there's a shift change," Charlie said as the stream of miners leaving the main shaft building grew in volume and headed for the cook shack.

"Look at them," said Pedro, his voice resonant with outrage. "They are treated worse than slaves."

Watching the miners, Fargo made up his mind. They were not going to be satisfied with just looting the company store. They were going to free those poor devils and destroy this mine.

"When it gets dark," Fargo told them, "I'll see if I can get inside the sleeping quarters. They should have a lot to tell me. And if I can bring them the means for escape . . ."

"Like files for their chains," suggested Pedro.

"Yes," agreed Fargo.

Charlie groaned. "I got files aplenty, but they're back in that wagon."

"I will go back for them," Rita told him.

Fargo turned quickly to her. "That won't be an easy trip. You sure you want to chance it?"

"I will get the files," she insisted.

"I'll saddle the mule for you," said Charlie, "and explain where to find the files."

A moment later the two had disappeared back into the gorge. Glancing back at the mine, Fargo became aware that the steady pounding of the stamping machine had not eased once since they came in sight of this mine. He looked over at Pedro.

"When I'm seeing to the miners, Pedro, you slip into that building over the shaft and fire the building. Tear up those engines, too, but make sure you haul the miners out of the shaft first."

Pedro nodded. "*Sí*, I know what you want," he said. "And maybe when miners are all safe, I cut cables, too."

Fargo nodded. "Yes. And with the pumps shut down, the mine's drifts and crosscuts will flood completely." He grinned at Pedro. "That ought to put a real crimp in Hawk Fletcher's operation."

Darkness fell swiftly. Soon the corners of the buildings and the trestles leading from the mine shaft were illuminated by gas lamps, which sent a pale light over the valley floor and the buildings clustered about the shaft.

Fargo had figured which building served as the saloon and gambling hall frequented by the men running the mine. It was a long building set up on pilings, with a porch that ran one length of it. Every time its door swung open, Fargo could hear the tinkle of a piano coming from within and the shrill laughter of women. Off-duty mine employees staggered out of the place periodically, sometimes singing off-key as they picked their way carefully down the wooden stairs and tailed off toward the barracks, another smaller building close by.

Charlie appeared beside him, muttering.

"That's a long climb Rita's got ahead of her," he told Fargo unhappily. "I should've gone with her."

"She'll be all right," Fargo assured him, sounding more confident than he felt.

Then he pointed out to Charlie the two buildings he had been studying, the saloon and the barracks behind it. Charlie should be able to torch both buildings when the time came.

Charlie grinned at him. "You want to destroy this place completely, huh?"

"That's right, Charlie. But there's women in the saloon," he cautioned, "so wait until there's enough excitement to draw them out of the place before you torch it."

"Meanwhile, you'll be cleaning out the store?"

"That's right," Fargo replied.

"We're goin' to be awful busy," Charlie commented happily.

Pedro said nothing. He just took out his knife and began strapping the blade on his sleeve.

*   *   *

A little before midnight, Rita returned with the files, and another item Charlie had requested she bring him as well: a small pickax. Charlie grabbed the mean-looking tool eagerly and took a few short, vicious jabs with it.

"This should do the job," he told Fargo, grinning.

"Rita," Fargo said, sticking the files she had handed him into his jacket's side pocket, "we need you to cover us when we start back to this gorge. We'll be moving fast and ducking lead, more than likely. It'll be up to you to keep those bastards off our backs—or we'll never make it. Think you can handle that?"

She nodded quickly. "I am good shot," she told Fargo. "You will see. Besides, do you not remember how Pedro and I cut down them Comanches?"

"I remember," Fargo replied, smiling. "Okay, then. The job's yours."

Fargo had been afraid Rita would insist on going with them, and was pleased she had taken his suggestion as easily as she had.

Fargo turned then to Charlie and Pedro. "Give me a chance to reach the miners' barracks before you move out. And stay low until I go for the company store. I expect all hell to break loose when I get there. That should create enough of a diversion to cover you both."

Charlie and Pedro nodded. Checking his Colt and knife, Fargo nodded quickly to the three of them and slipped away into the night.

Coming upon the miners' sleeping quarters from the rear, Fargo peered in through the narrow, barred

65

windows. It took a while for his eyes to grow accustomed to the darkness, but with the light from outside filtering into the long room, he managed finally to make out the interior.

Cots lined both walls. In front of the cots along the floor, Fargo saw two long cables running the length of the room. They appeared to pass through steel loops fastened to the floor, and it was to the master cables that those manacles hobbling the cots' occupants were fastened.

The miners were reclining on their cots, a few sitting up and whispering to others near them. Most of them, however, were trying to sleep, despite their restlessness, and their bodies—covered only with ragged sheets or blankets—tossed and turned on their narrow cots, the sound of their chinking chains coming through the window to Fargo.

Beside each cot was a filthy chamber pot. How the men managed to use it, chained as they were to the cables, was a mystery to Fargo. The floors around the slops jars were littered with night soil. Fargo could smell the stench emanating from the place even through the dirt-encrusted pane of glass.

There were no guards inside the room. There was not a white man alive who would accept such a post, Fargo realized grimly.

The windows were all barred and were too narrow to admit a grown man through, in any case. The only way into the sleeping quarters was the door leading off the front porch. Fargo moved away from the window, circled the building until he was standing in the shadows alongside the porch.

On each side of the door two guards were stationed, slumped back into wooden chairs propped against the wall, shotguns across their laps. From where he stood—about fifteen feet away—Fargo could just catch the soft murmur of their conversation. Their boots were resting on the porch railing while they discussed one of the girls in the saloon. It was clear their present occupation bored them.

Fargo bent and selected a rock with the heft he preferred, and threw the stone high, intending it to come down near the opposite corner of the building. He threw it perfectly and the rock struck the side of the building before bounding out toward the street. Both men tipped their chairs forward onto the porch and sat up. The guard farthest from Fargo got to his feet, curious, and craned his neck to look in the direction from which the sound had come.

"What in hell was that?" he asked.

"Sounded like a rock."

The man standing looked across the street. He cupped a hand to his mouth, and cried, "Someone over there tryin' to cook up a storm, maybe?"

His companion, still sitting, looked across the street and grinned. "If that's you, Jim," he cried, "we're ready for you!"

When there was no response from across the street, the first guard, still on his feet, walked down the porch until he reached the corner of the building. Leaning his shotgun against the wall, he peered over the railing. Then he walked to the front of the porch and stared into the darkness.

"I could've sworn I heard something," he called back to his companion.

"You did. I heard it too."

"Maybe it was bats."

Placing the blade of his bowie between his teeth, Fargo grabbed the top of the railing and vaulted up onto the porch, landing as soundlessly as a cat. Out of the corner of his eye, the guard still in the chair caught the movement and turned to stare at him. Fargo threw his knife. The blade buried itself in the guard's throat below the Adam's apple, shutting off any possibility of a scream.

Hearing the guard's shotgun slam to the porch floor, the other flung himself around. Seeing Fargo, he started for his shotgun. But Fargo had already grabbed the fallen shotgun, and in three swift strides he was close enough to swing the heavy double barrel, catching the guard on the side of the head.

The guard went down on one knee, groaning, his hand held up to his shattered skull. Hurrying back for his knife, Fargo returned to him and slit his throat. Ignoring the warm blood that poured from the guard's jugular, Fargo dragged him across the porch to his chair and propped him back up into it.

The other guard had remained slumped in his chair. Fargo tipped both chairs back against the wall, slapped the guards' hats back onto their heads, took the key ring from the first guard, and found the key that unlocked the door's huge padlock. Unlocking it, Fargo threw the padlock aside and lifted down a wooden beam fitted across the door.

He pushed the door open. The stench was awesome. He paused a moment; then, picking up the dead guards' two shotguns, he stepped into the miners' sleeping quarters and closed the door behind him.

"Anyone here speak English?" he called, leaning the two shotguns against the wall.

"Over here," a white-haired, frail-looking fellow told him from the far corner. "But I ain't gonna be much help," he sniffed, his tone an unpleasant, grating whine. "A cave-in done ruined my leg. I'm a cripple. I can't walk no more."

"Can you talk these Indians' lingo?"

"I can."

"Then tell them I came to free them."

"You some crazy Quaker, mister? Leave these here Indians be."

"Didn't you hear what I said?"

"I heard you," the cripple said, his voice nasty now, threatening. "You better get out of here. If you don't, I'll let the guards know what you're up to."

Fargo stalked over to him, furious. "You do that, you bastard, and you'll be the first to die." Fargo took out his Colt. "Now, do as I say. Tell these here Indians I'm here to free them."

"I will like hell," the cripple said defiantly. "You wouldn't dare shoot me. If you did, you'd bring all the guards."

"Never mind him," said a huge Indian sitting up on his cot to Fargo's right. "I speak English good. I tell other Indian what you say."

"All right," Fargo snapped, moving quickly over to him. "Do it!"

By this time the commotion had awakened all the miners, and most of them were sitting up on their cots staring at Fargo. A dim, confused mutter ran up and down the room. The Ute silenced them with a sharp command, then boomed out Fargo's intentions. Though Fargo couldn't understand a word, it was clear they understood that their deliverance was at hand. When the Ute finished, they quieted down and waited, hushed and expectant.

"Fine," said Fargo, stepping closer to the big Ute. "Here's a file. Use this to cut through those chains on your feet. Then help the others."

The Ute had shoulders as broad as an open barn door and a dark, fierce countenance that looked as if it had been hacked out of stone. Grabbing the file from Fargo, he began filing away at the chains binding his left ankle. Fargo told him to keep the chains, since they would have to serve as weapons.

Feeling somewhat easier about the operation now, Fargo passed out files to the other captives, then went back to see how the big Indian was doing. The Indian's strength was prodigious. Already he had filed through the links attaching the chain to his left ankle.

"What are you called?" Fargo asked him.

"Buffalo Wallow."

"I am called Skye Fargo."

The Indian grunted and continued to file on the links to his right ankle. He did not miss a stroke or look up.

"I need your help," Fargo told him.

Without looking up, the Indian said, "Buffalo Wallow will help. If this big trick, he will kill you. If not, you will see gratitude of Ute Indian."

"Where'd you learn English?"

"Missionary teach me," he grunted. "He is crazy man. Says earth is bad, death is good. He also blame devil for many bad things. I blame white man. And maybe sometime, Indian."

Abruptly, he stood up, yanking his right leg free. He took a deep breath and looked about him, his black eyes gleaming like wet anthracite, his enormous shoulders appearing to swell to even greater dimensions. His entire body seemed to grow more powerful and unconfined. He was a man set loose after a long and terrible imprisonment, and Fargo remembered a story he had heard once of a giant genie who, after having been released from a bottle after centuries of confinement, threatened to kill the man responsible for his freedom.

Instead, Buffalo Wallow moved off down the row of cots to help the others file through their chains.

Fargo moved over to one of the front windows to peer out. The mining camp was still perfectly quiet. The gas lamps flickered on the sides of the buildings and on the skeletal underpinnings of the ore trestle. Over the entire valley, with metronomic consistency, the shuddering beat of the stamping mill continued without pause.

Buffalo Wallow appeared beside him. Fargo turned. Behind the Indian stood the ranks of the freed brothers and the few whites who had been working with them—a ragged, stinking army that looked as if it had just emerged, unbidden, from the bowels of hell. Dangling from each of their fists, Fargo noted, were their sundered chains.

"We free now," said Buffalo Wallow, his voice powerful even in a whisper. "We ready to go. The one with rotten leg will stay."

Fargo turned to look in that direction. He saw the cripple's dim figure sprawled awkwardly back upon his cot.

"I kill him with chain." A bleak smile lightened the big Indian's features.

Fargo looked at the big Indian closely. It appeared that Buffalo Wallow had taken the opportunity to settle an old score. And why not?

"All right," Fargo said, speaking softly to Buffalo Wallow. "All of you can go now if you want. But I need help in breaking into that company store across the yard. There should be plenty ammunition and provisions in there, and I need both."

"I will go with you," Buffalo Wallow told Fargo.

"Can you get any more to help us?"

"How many you want?"

"Ten."

Buffalo Wallow turned and quickly selected ten of the strongest-looking braves. The rest—it looked like close to fifteen—he waved toward the door. Fargo opened the door and stepped back. Moving like shadows, the Utes dropped off the porch and vanished into the night, their chains clinking softly as they moved. Fargo shuddered. He sure as hell wouldn't want to be any white guard they ran into this night.

Fargo took one of the two shotguns he had taken

from the guards and handed the other to Buffalo Wallow.

"It's loaded," he said. "Let's go."

Fargo went first, darting across the porch and down the steps, Buffalo Wallow and the ten Utes keeping close behind him. They were almost to the company store when two men appeared from around the corner of the building.

Both of them wore large sombreros and, to keep off the high country's chill, ponchos that extended down to their knees. From the look of them, they were Mexicans. Both had whiskey bottles in their hands, and when they saw Fargo and the others trotting through the night toward them, they pulled up in astonishment.

Their delay was fatal. As they dropped their bottles and clawed for their sidewarms, Fargo blasted the nearest one, the load of double-0 shot almost cutting him in half. A split second later Buffalo Wallow took out the other one.

The two blasts exploded the silence. Instantly, it seemed, doors and windows were flung open, flooding the ground with stripes of light. Cries of alarm were sounded, and the night was filled suddenly with the sound of running feet and shouting voices.

Waving his men on to the store, Fargo and Buffalo Wallow took only a moment to batter their way through the door. As they poured into the store, Fargo lit a couple of lamps. On one wall near the counter, rifles were on display. New ones, it appeared. Henry repeaters. Behind the counter they found boxes of ammunition. Fargo began handing out the rifles and ammunition as fast as he could, while outside, the night came alive with the ragged cries of men dying violently. The Indians Fargo had just freed were evidently moving through the night and using their chains.

Buffalo Wallow had flung away his shotgun and was now proudly carrying a repeater, his pockets bulging with boxes of cartridges. Smiling, he held up the rifle for Fargo to see.

"It is so new I smell oil from packing," the big Indian told Fargo. "Many white bastards I kill with this. Then I return to my people and hunt. This is good night."

Fargo had gotten himself a Henry as well and plenty of ammunition. He took two extra Henrys for Charlie and Pedro, and as much ammunition as he could carry. They would need this firepower later when they reached Hell Town.

"I'm going to get a wagon to haul the provisions," Fargo told Buffalo Wallow. "But I'll need some of your men to help me load it. Then you and the others can go."

"What provisions you want?"

Fargo told him.

"I will see to it."

As the Indians began dragging from the store-rooms the grain, sugar, and canned goods Fargo had requested, Fargo went to the doorway and peered out.

Gunfire was increasing in frequency all around him, along with startled shouts and cries of terror that were usually cut off with a suddenness that sent a chill up Fargo's spine. Abruptly a series of shots came from the darkness near one of the mine buildings as tiny geysers of dirt began exploding at Fargo's feet. A moment later the rounds were slamming into the wall beside him.

Crouching low, Fargo lifted his Henry and sent a quick fusilade into the shadows, aiming a little above the spot where he had seen the gun flashes. The return fire ceased, and Fargo saw two men running off.

Fargo ducked back inside the store and found Buffalo Wallow. "We don't have much more time. Stay here and keep a lookout. I'm going for the wagon."

Slipping out through the rear door, Fargo trotted through the night to the stable. Swiftly hitching up two workhorses to a wagon, he drove it back to the store, keeping his head down as the rattle of gunfire grew in volume all around him.

As soon as he pulled to a halt in front of the store, the Indians began loading up the provisions they had taken from the shelves and storerooms.

Abruptly, a titanic explosion rocked the valley.

Glancing over, Fargo saw the buildings over the mine shaft disintegrating into a towering ball of fire. That would be Pedro's doing, he knew. But where in hell had he got the explosives?

A second later Fargo saw men and women streaming from the saloon and gambling hall just as the saloon itself and the barracks behind it went up in flames. Fargo knew that was the handiwork of Charlie Kettle. The old-timer was right on schedule, too.

Fargo hurried back inside the store. Snatching up brooms, he wrapped towels and blankets around the straw and ducked into the back room, where he had noticed barrels of kerosene. Turning on the spigots, he filled four cans with the kerosene to be loaded onto the wagon, then saturated the makeshift torches. Handing them out to the Indians, he pressed upon them at the same time boxes of sulfur matches.

"Light these torches and set every building you can reach on fire," he told them. "Burn this whole damn pesthole to the ground."

Their eyes alight, the Indians fanned out from the store.

That left Fargo and Buffalo Wallow to finish loading the wagon. When they had done so, Fargo went back inside the store. Picking up one of the lanterns he had lit, he walked into the back room and hurled it against the side of the kerosene barrel. The still-flowing kerosene caught in a single, massive blast that almost knocked Fargo off his feet. He ran from the store and clambered up onto the seat beside Buffalo Wallow.

"Let's get the hell out of here," he told him.

The Indian slapped the reins hard, letting out a war cry that raised the hair on Fargo's scalp. The horses took the bit as if they were flying from the mouth of hell, forcing Fargo to grab hold of his seat.

They had not left the store a moment too soon. Two riders galloped out of the hellish night and began to overtake them, firing as they came. But in the light from the burning store, the horsemen were outlined clearly. Flinging up his Colt, Fargo took out the nearest rider, then levered a shell into his Henry and cut down the second one.

As the wagon plunged on through the night, Fargo found himself well pleased with his new rifle.

6

Without further challenge they reached the entrance to the gorge. As Fargo jumped down from the wagon, Rita appeared from behind the rocks. She was holding Fargo's Sharps.

"Are you all right?" she asked Fargo.

"Not a scratch," he replied.

She looked up at the big Indian almost timidly. His great dark eyes regarded her somberly.

"Meet Buffalo Wallow," he told her.

The Indian bowed his head slightly.

"This here is Rita," Fargo told the Indian. "Her brother is out there now, doing what he can to bring this mine to a halt."

"He do fine," the Indian told Rita, turning his attention back to the blazing buildings near the mine shaft.

Fargo looked back as well.

It was something to watch. He could occasionally

pick out Indians racing through the night with the torches Fargo had given them. By this time every major building in the valley had been touched off, plus the sheds and buildings over the mine shaft.

"Look!" Rita cried, pointing.

It was the trestle that carried the ore carts to the crushing mills. As the flames licked at its fragile network of supporting beams, the tracks began to sag, then buckle. A moment later, the entire network collapsed, sending the carts plunging into the flames.

"I just think of something," Rita said, frowning in concentration as she tipped her head slightly. "I do not hear the crushers anymore."

"And neither will this valley," Fargo told her. "For a good long while. Pedro's doing a fine job."

Buffalo Wallow grunted and pointed.

Out of the hellish night, about ten or fifteen riders were galloping toward them. These were all that remained of the engineers and overseers who had been running the mine, Fargo realized. Armed with repeating rifles, they began firing before they were within range of the entrance to the gorge.

"Drive the wagon farther back," Fargo told Rita as he and Buffalo Wallow settled down behind some boulders. "And keep your head down."

The riders came on in a bunch, too enraged to think clearly and spread out. Fargo opened fire as soon as he could be sure of doing some damage. It turned into a turkey shoot. As Fargo and Buffalo blazed away, the riders slowed, then broke ranks. When at last they lost heart, wheeled, and broke back the way they had come, there were only six or seven men still on their mounts.

"Damn fools," Fargo muttered.

Not long after, Charlie Kettle, half-carrying Pedro, emerged from the darkness. Rita uttered a cry of concern and rushed to Charlie's side to help him with her brother. Pedro smiled weakly and tried to brush her off. When he caught sight of Fargo, a proud smile creased his dark, handsome face.

"Do not worry, Fargo," he gasped. "All miners, they get out sure enough. But the mine is finished."

"Where the hell did you get the dynamite to blow it?"

"Plenty boxes lie all around. The miners, they help me set charges."

"You sure did a great job," said Charlie, looking back at the blazing buildings. "Reminds me of the Fourth of July. Only more so."

The entire valley was now an inferno as the walls of the mountains flanking the valley appeared to keep in the heat, concentrating it terribly. In fact, the flames devouring the mining complex were so bright that the slopes stood out as bright as day, revealing the terrible erosion near the valley floor as well as the green islands of pine close to the top.

Watching the flames, Fargo remembered Conchita and his promise to her. He was beginning to gain a dim consciousness of how he would deal with Hawk Fletcher and his Hell Town when the time came.

Out of the flames devilish figures darted toward them, gleaming from the perspiration covering their bronzed bodies. Some were still brandishing the stumps of the torches Fargo had fashioned for them along with the rifles they had taken from the store, and from more than a few belts Fargo saw the damp locks of freshly taken scalps.

Behind them galloped more, riding horses bareback as they drove before them at least twenty or thirty horses they had rescued from the blazing stables.

When they reached the entrance to the gorge, they realized that they were from that moment on free, no longer chained slaves belonging to the mine owners. They began dancing about like overgrown children as they brandished their weapons and leapt aboard those horses that had been taken.

Fargo shared in their joy as he watched the Indians' celebration. He was so engrossed he did not hear Rita approaching him. She took his arm and pulled him urgently back from the shouting, animated crush of Indians.

"What is it, Rita?"

"It is Pedro! He was wounded worse than he say. In the side. He try not to let me see it. But I think it is bad, Skye. Very bad."

Fargo grabbed Charlie and together they followed Rita to a quiet spot farther up into the gorge beside the stream. Pedro was lying down on the grass. In the pale light from the stars, he looked weak and fragile.

Examining the wound, Fargo saw at once how bad it was.

"The bullet still inside?" he asked Pedro.

"I think so," Pedro replied, moistening dry lips,

perspiration coursing down his face. The young man was obviously in great pain.

Charlie shook his head. "That bullet will have to come out."

"Then go ahead, Charlie. Take it out."

"I ain't got no light. I'll have to wait until tomorrow morning." Charlie turned to Fargo. "And besides that, we got to get back up to my wagon. I got a bag with some surgical instruments in it."

"We'll start now."

Fargo went back and explained things to Buffalo Wallow, fully expecting the big Indian to begin pulling out at once with his fellow Utes.

Instead, the big Indian began issuing orders like a deranged fireman, and before Fargo or Charlie could stop them, the Indians had hoisted onto their backs the wagon Fargo had taken from the mine's stable, along with its provisions, and were climbing up the side of the gorge, heading for the spot where Charlie had been forced to leave his own wagon.

Behind the wagon they carried Pedro.

Fashioning a crude stretcher, the Indians hauled the injured Pedro up through the gorge, Fargo, Charlie, and Rita following behind.

It was dawn before they reached the rim of the gorge and full light when they halted beside Charlie's wagon. At once Charlie had the Indians put Pedro down on the wagon's bed. He peeled back the canvas for light, opened his medicine bag, and went probing for the slug in Pedro's side. While the old man worked, a silent, awed circle of Indians enclosed the wagon.

Charlie was not very gentle; he was an old man and not a legitimate doctor. But Pedro did not utter a sound. Not until Charlie held up the slug for all to see and washed out Pedro's wound with raw whiskey, did Pedro sigh and reach out for his sister's hand.

She squeezed it and hung on to it as Charlie finished bandaging up the young man's side.

"He'll be fit as a mountain lion once he gets enough rest," Charlie proclaimed, hopping down from the wagon and grabbing the bottle of whiskey. He gulped down half its contents, then punched the cork back into it, his face dark with a concern he did not let Rita see.

An hour later, with Pedro asleep in the back of Charlie's wagon, Fargo pulled the anxious Rita to one side.

"You'll have to take him back to Bent Rock," Fargo told her.

"Yes," she said. "I was thinking that."

"You can use the wagon we took from the mine," he told her. "It won't be an easy journey, but we'll give you plenty of provisions. Just take it easy and you'll be all right."

"I wanted very much to kill this Fletcher."

"I'll do it for you."

"Just you, Fargo? That is crazy."

"It's surprising what one determined man can accomplish. Look at that mine shaft. Pedro did quite a job on it."

"Yes," she said, brightening. "He did." She looked

intently up at Fargo then. "Will you return to Bent Rock? Will I see you again?"

"Sure. If I can. The job wouldn't be complete if I didn't report to you what happened."

"Is that a promise?"

He nodded. "That's a promise. Now I suggest you get a move on. Charlie and Buffalo Wallow are piling the provisions you'll need into the wagon right now. And those two horses look pretty healthy to me."

She nodded. "Thank you, Fargo."

He started to turn away.

"Fargo?"

He paused and looked back. Rita flung her arms about his neck and kissed him passionately on the lips. "That is so you will remember me," she told him. "And keep your promise to come back."

He smiled at her. "I told you. I will if I can."

As Rita's wagon vanished back along the trail, Fargo turned to Buffalo Wallow, who had been standing with Charlie, watching.

"You should be on your way now, too, Buffalo Wallow," Fargo told him. "Back to your own people. With gifts to make their eyes light up."

"Where Skye Fargo and the white-haired man go now?"

"After the son of a bitch who set up this mine."

"You know who this is?"

"A Comanchero," Fargo told him. "Hawk Fletcher. He's got a town somewhere in these mountains. We aim to find it."

"That not be easy. Comancheros have treaty with Comanche."

"I know that."

"You no care?" Buffalo Wallow asked, surprised.

"No."

The big Indian smiled. "Then Buffalo Wallow no care. He go with Skye Fargo."

"You?"

The Indian nodded. "And other Indian, too."

"Now there ain't no need for you and your people to do that," protested Charlie. "You done helped us enough."

"I promise them much plunder." He smiled. "Even if no plunder, it will be good to wring Comanchero necks. It is Comanchero who raid my people's villages and bring them to this mine."

"Well, now," said Fargo, not at all displeased at this news, "you don't have to twist my arms any to make me bring you along, Buffalo. I guess maybe you got as good a reason as we have for bringing this bastard and his men down."

Charlie said, "Hey, Buffalo, you wouldn't happen to know where in blazes this Hell Town is, would you? We been scratchin' all over this pile of stone and pine without much luck."

Buffalo Wallow nodded. "I know," he said.

"How far is it from here?"

"Two, maybe three days' ride."

Charlie looked at Fargo, beaming. "Well, now, Fargo, what do you think of them apples?"

Smiling, Fargo turned to the big Indian. "Thanks, Buffalo. We really appreciate it."

"Hell's bells. You no need thank me. I thank you. You take chains off Buffalo Wallow and his people. You make us free. Now we breathe again mountain air. Never again will we be in chains. Never again will we go deep into the ground to dig in the rivers of hell."

"I hope so, Buffalo Wallow."

"Come now. I choose those who ride with us. Then we divide horses." As he said this last, his anthracite eyes glowed eagerly.

Fargo understood why. As the horses had been driven into the gorge and herded up its steep sides, Fargo had seen the big Indian studying closely one powerful chestnut in particular, the largest saddle horse in the gather.

Fargo had no doubt who would get that horse.

7

Two days later they came down through a pass and found themselves crossing a high parkland, lush with grass and cut with icy streams, the scent of wildflowers and sage heavy in the air.

Even with Rita and her brother gone, Fargo and his allies were a sizable force. Charlie Kettle still had only the single mule pulling his wagon, but the animal seemed content enough, despite the additional load of provisions and weapons it held. Riding ahead of the wagon were Fargo and Buffalo Wallow; the ten Ute Indians kept a loose formation to the sides and rear.

The farther into the parkland they rode, Fargo noticed, the more distant and remote became the encircling snow-capped peaks. Glancing around at them, Fargo drew alongside Buffalo Wallow.

"This sure as hell is pretty country, Buffalo."

"This is land of crazy man," the Indian responded, his big round face mournful.

"What do you mean by that?"

Buffalo Wallow pointed straight ahead. "Soon we come to cottonwoods and pines. There is big house. It belong to crazy rancher. He bring in many cattle and build big house with stone chimney. He bring woman and soon have one child. He think he all right here. I tell him this is Comanchero country, but he not listen. Instead, he pat his gun and invite me in for coffee. When I leave, he give me fine gift."

"That doesn't make him crazy. What'd he give you?"

"Fine gold watch. It is in my lodge now. I wind it and hear it tick. Sometimes it keep me awake." He smiled suddenly. "It chimes, too. It has very small voice. All children crowd in to hear it. My woman call me He Who Worship Watch."

"Why?"

"She say I look at it before I leave in morning and when I come back at night."

Fargo chuckled. Maybe Buffalo Wallow's woman had a point. "Well, if we have time, Buffalo Wallow, we may stop at this rancher's place. How far ahead is it?"

"It not far. We get there by sundown."

"When's the last time you saw the rancher?"

"I not see him in many moons. I am not like crazy rancher. Until this time I stay out of Comanchero country."

"What's his name?"

"Riley. He tell me call him Mike."

"I'll bet he's got red hair."

"How you know that?"

"Just sounds like it," Fargo said.

At a distance, planted in amid a towering grove of cottonwoods, Mike Riley's two-story ranch house was as impressive as Buffalo Wallow had indicated it would be.

Until Fargo got closer.

With each passing moment, his apprehension grew. It was sunset and some of the windows reflected the bright sky overhead, but not all of them. Those that didn't were lacking glass. The porch was grand enough and covered the entire front portion of the house, but thick, choking grass had grown so high the porch floor was almost completely hidden, and most of the railing had been taken over by creepers.

The fieldstone fireplace, covering one end of the house, was still intact, but a portion of the roof was missing, and Fargo could see the black beams still spanning the gaping hole. By this time, the chill evening breeze carried the smell of charred walls, woodwork, furniture, mattresses, and all the countless items that had never been meant to feel the terrible annihilation of flames. It was, Fargo thought, the saddest smell of all—that of old dreams and old hopes, forever dead.

Skirting a couple of towering cottonwoods, they came in sight of the front of the house. Windows on the first and second floor were now empty, staring sockets, and the front door was wide open, enabling Fargo to glimpse the black emptiness within. As they approached the house, Fargo felt he was looking at the face of a demented man staring mindlessly, unseeingly back at him.

Buffalo Wallow grunted unhappily. Fargo said nothing. He knew what the Indian must be thinking. And feeling. Fargo felt it himself—a heavy, sick knot in the pit of his stomach.

"I know it is bad when I see no cattle," Buffalo Wallow said. "But I hope cattle in far pasture for now."

They were inside the ranch compound by this time, riding alongside a crumbling barn, its foundation lost in weeds. Behind the barn Fargo glimpsed a sorrel. It looked healthy enough, but not well-cared-for.

A shot rang out and Fargo lost his hat. Fargo dived off his pinto, Buffalo Wallow following his example. Crouching behind his wagon, Charlie cried, "Don't fire! We're friends! Don't fire!"

Crouching in the deep grass Fargo heard the Utes wheel their horses and fan out swiftly, taking cover in the cottonwoods. But there was no more shooting. Just a waiting, prolonged silence. With his Colt cocked, Fargo slowly stood up and looked around. The shot had come from a cluster of buildings ahead of him—what was left of a blacksmith shop and a small, nearly overgrown bunkhouse. But there were no more shots. Fargo picked up his hat, inspected the hole in it, then slapped it angrily back onto his head.

"Riley," Fargo cried. "Goddammit! Hold your fire! We ain't Comancheros. Can't you tell that?"

That did it.

Mike Riley came out of the bunkhouse and walked slowly toward them, his rifle held at the ready. His red hair had grown down clear to his shoulders, where it met his equally red beard. Fargo caught a glimpse of squinting, wary green eyes just above raw cheekbones. His clothes were filthy and hung on his gaunt frame in tatters. The hat he wore had lost part of its rim, and a filthy kerchief was knotted at his neck.

Less than fifty yards away he pulled up.

"Who in hell are you?" he demanded, his voice a painful rasp. "And what're you doin' on my land?"

That was when Fargo noticed the scars on his neck. They looked like rope burns.

"We're just passing through," Fargo explained. "Thought you might let us light and set a spell."

"Can't you see?"

"Yeah," agreed Fargo, looking past Riley at the house. "I can see. Sorry we bothered you."

"Now wait a minute, dammit. Don't go off like that." Riley lowered his rifle and moved closer.

As he did so, the Indians, still mounted, moved out of the cottonwoods and rode slowly closer, their rifles resting across the necks of their mounts. Seeing this, Riley pulled up, alarmed.

"No worry," said Buffalo Wallow to Riley. "They Ute Indians. They friendly."

Riley peered with sudden intentness at Buffalo Wallow, and suddenly a light of recognition spread over his bearded face. He walked up to the big Indian and stuck out his hand.

"You came back, old friend," Riley said, shaking the Indian's huge hand vigorously. Then he looked at Fargo. "Come ahead. All of you. We'll go in the house,

I ain't got much 'cept coffee, some bacon, and beans, but you're welcome to what's there."

"In the house?" Fargo asked, not certain Riley meant what he had just said.

"It's all right," Riley explained. "There's rooms in there ain't too bad. The kitchen's gone, but I only use the living room now anyway."

With Mike Riley leading them, Fargo's motley army tramped in through the open door, through a blackened hallway and on into the main living room, the only room in the house that still boasted four walls.

A single wooden cabinet sat in a corner beside the chimney. In front of the huge fieldstone fireplace there was a crude table and chairs and a roughly constructed easy chair with dusty blankets thrown over the back and the armrests. In one corner sat a foulsmelling slops jar, and around the fireplace, fragments of food littered the bare floor. A pile of filthy blankets in another corner indicated where Mike Riley slept. On two of the windows were curtains still hung, the only two windows that still held unbroken panes of glass.

The food Riley had promised them he pulled out of the wooden cabinet by the fireplace. It didn't look all that well-preserved, but no one said a word as Riley built up the fire in the fireplace, spooned coffee into his coffeepot, and set it down in the fire. He dropped strips of bacon on huge platters, dumped out the contents of four cans of beans alongside them, and thrust the platters close to the now-blazing fire.

Then he waved Fargo and Charlie over to the table. "Sit down," he said. "Make yourselves comfortable."

Since there were only four chairs, Fargo, Charlie, and Buffalo Wallow sat up at the table, leaving Buffalo Wallow's Indian cavalry to make themselves as comfortable as they could on the floor, a task they accomplished with considerable dignity.

Riley did not eat himself. He was content to sip his coffee and watch everyone else eat. The platter of bacon and beans was passed to the Indians after Fargo, Charlie, and Buffalo Wallow took from it the smallest possible portions. When the platter finished making its rounds, Fargo was pleased to note how completely it had been picked clean.

Three pots of coffee later, Riley looked at Buffalo Wallow and said, "You warned me."

Buffalo Wallow nodded somberly, his impassive face grave.

"You said I was crazy to build here. And then bring my stock in and my wife. You said the Comancheros ruled this land." Riley's eyes were bleak with sudden grief. "But I didn't believe you. Instead, I gave you a gift—a pocket watch. You had admired it, I remembered."

"I have it still," said Buffalo Wallow gravely.

Riley looked at Fargo and Charlie. "You see, I thought he was just a simple savage, so I didn't take his warning seriously. Then I rode out one afternoon to gather some calves from the upper pasture, and when I returned, the Comancheros were here, milling about in the front yard and looting."

Tears welled up in his eyes, but at the same time they gained such a look of wild intensity Fargo was riveted.

93

"Sarah, my wife, was lying on the grass in front of the door. Her skirt was over her head and her under-garments had been ripped off. She was bloody where they took her, and her arms were spread wide, like a large rag doll. When I called her name, she didn't answer. She was dead, thank God. My daughter, Charity, was up on a horse with one of the Coman-cheros, crying. She called to me. I went to get her, and they struck me down like I was a stalk of hay. Before they left, they fired the house and strung me up from a cottonwood. I twisted slowly while it rained steadily, putting out the flames."

Riley paused. Fargo said nothing. There was nothing—absolutely nothing—for him *to* say. Through the years, the long years of tracking and searching, he had heard other, similar stories. And the memory of Conchita's recent death was still raw in his memory. Yet Riley's account chilled him clear to the marrow.

"My neck refused to break," Riley continued. "So I reached up and pulled myself onto the limb. Once there, I was able to loosen the noose and drop to the ground. My horse had earlier bolted to the hills. A few days later it returned. I have been waiting ever since."

"What are you waiting for?" Charlie asked.

"For them to come back. I am sure they will return. And when they do, I will kill them."

"Just you alone?"

"Yes. The way I almost killed you."

In that moment it blazed out at them from his eyes—the frenzied light of madness. Fargo looked away quickly and saw that both Charlie and Buffalo Wallow had also seen the madness in Riley's eyes.

"You'd better go back," said Riley.

"Why?"

"The Comancheros."

"No. We're goin' on—after them," drawled Charlie.

Riley's eyes narrowed. "Yes. There are many of you."

"And we're well-armed."

"You must know where they are."

"Hell Town," replied Fargo.

"Yes. Devils from the bowels of hell, they are. I have seen them in the trees at night, watching me. They have horns and a tail. But they dare not come any closer than the trees."

Fargo got to his feet. "Thanks for the meal and the coffee, Riley. We'd like to make camp in your cotton-woods, if you don't mind."

"It is dangerous," Riley said. "I told you. They are out there."

"We'll set out sentries."

Riley nodded briskly. "Excellent idea. That is what I should have done. But they were waiting when I got back, you see."

Fargo glanced at Charlie and Buffalo Wallow, then started from the room. As the two followed him, the Indians got up from the floor and filed out after them. Just before Fargo stepped out into the dusk, he glanced back and saw Riley still sitting at the table, staring straight ahead of him, the flames in the fire-place reflecting wildly in his eyes.

When Fargo awoke the next morning, he found Riley standing over him, watching him closely.

"I didn't want to wake you," Riley said.

Fargo sat up and reached for his hat. Throwing aside the flap of his soogan, he began to pull on his boots. "That's all right, Riley."

"I have coffee waiting. And bacon. It's ready now."

"Much obliged."

The breakfast was the same as the evening meal, only this time when Fargo and the others were finished, they left the house quickly, anxious to be on their way.

Riley and his ruin of a house had sent shivers to the roots of each man's soul—Indian and white alike.

They were mounted up and moving out through the cottonwoods when Riley came out to bid them good-bye. Or so they thought.

Fargo pulled his pinto to a halt and waited.

"I want to go with you," said Riley.

"You shouldn't leave your place."

He smiled thinly. "What is there here for me?"

Fargo looked for a long moment at the ragged man before him. A man's got a right to avenge the horror he's suffered, Fargo figured.

"How long will it take to get your things?"

"I have all I need here," he said, patting his holstered Colt and hefting his rifle. "I'll get my horse."

Not long after, as they rode back out through the cottonwoods, Fargo glanced back one last time at the ruined ranch house. Like sad, accusing eyes, the broken windows seemed to follow them.

Riley, Fargo noticed, did not look back.

For a man teetering on the brink of madness, Riley was little bother. He kept his counsel and it was soon obvious he was an excellent rider. Early on the second day, he rode out ahead of them and was soon ranging farther and farther afield until he paused on a knoll ahead of them, waved briefly, then vanished.

When they made noon camp, he still had not returned. Sipping his coffee, Charlie stepped over to Fargo and remarked on Riley's continued absence.

Fargo emptied his coffee cup and flung the dregs into the fire. "There's no law says he has to stay close by. But I admit it bothers me some."

"It bothers me too. But not these Indians. They know he's tetched; so as far as they're concerned, Riley's in tune with the Great White Spirit."

Fargo grinned and shrugged. "Hell, maybe they're right."

Buffalo Wallow came over, his big pan of a face somber. "I think I go find Riley," he said.

"You worried?"

"Maybe. We not too far now from Comanchero camp, I think."

"Go ahead," Fargo told him. "You know this country as well as I do."

"Now we lost two," grumbled Charlie as he watched the big Indian ride out. "Pretty soon, it'll just be the two of us left."

Fargo chuckled. "Don't fret, Charlie. That's all there was to begin with, remember? Besides, we can move on if we want. There's nothing says we have to stay here and wait for them."

Fargo squatted beside the fire and, reaching for the coffeepot, poured himself a fresh cup.

A half-hour later, when Buffalo Wallow did not return, they set off anyway, keeping to the same course they had followed since sunup. They were soon in wooded country, pines and aspen mostly, the timber spaced enough to enable them to ride on through it without much difficulty.

Fargo was the first to see Buffalo Wallow riding toward them, Riley close on his heels. They were not sparing their horses, either of them. Fargo slowed to a halt and Charlie hauled back on his mule's reins. The Indians halted their mounts close around Fargo and Charlie's wagon. They were as anxious as Fargo to learn why Buffalo Wallow and Riley were riding so hard to meet them.

"We see Comanches," Buffalo Wallow said as he brought his chestnut to a halt beside Fargo.

"Where?"

Riley pulled up on the other side of Fargo's pinto. "Just ahead of us on the other side of this timber."

"How many?"

"Big war party," said Buffalo Wallow. "They just come from Comanchero camp, I think. They have many fine new rifles. Whiskey too. Fire go out, they still dance. Many fall down."

"Can we take 'em?"

"Too many," Buffalo Wallow said. "Twenty, thirty—maybe more."

"We could lay low in this timber," said Charlie, "and wait till they move on."

Fargo glanced at him. "Sure. If we could be certain

they wouldn't find us. If they did while we were in here, we'd never get out. They'd pick us apart in a couple of days, like plucking berries in the springtime."

"So we attack?"

"No. We didn't come this far to fight Comanches. We'll get as close to them as we can, but stay in the timber. We'll fight if we have to, but as soon as it gets dark, we'll see if we can get around them."

Charlie shrugged. Fargo looked at Riley and Buffalo Wallow. When they offered no objection, Fargo took that as agreement and spurred his pinto on into the pines.

A few hours before midnight, with the Comanches camp sleeping off the rum they had consumed, Fargo and his party slipped across a moonlit patch of meadow less than a hundred yards above their encampment, then rode on into some rocks. A moment later they were descending through a steep canyon, loud with the sound of rushing water, each minute putting the Comanches farther behind them.

They kept going through the night and at dawn were riding through a thin stand of aspen when Buffalo Wallow held up suddenly. Fargo and the Indians behind him halted just as quickly.

"What is it?" Fargo asked the big Indian.

"There. Through the trees."

The sun had not risen high enough to burn off the heavy mists that now hung close over the meadowland, and through these mists rode a steady stream of

Comanches. They were heading directly toward Fargo and his party.

Fargo cursed bitterly. "These mountains have more Comanches than a dog has fleas."

"And they're gettin' closer, damn their red hides," said Charlie.

"Now we fight," said Buffalo Wallow, straightening eagerly on his mount. "We run no more."

Riley pulled his horse alongside Fargo's pinto. "It is the Comancheros you must fight," he said to both Fargo and Buffalo Wallow, "not this war party."

"Sure," said Charlie, standing up on his wagon seat and inspecting his rifle. "But first things first."

"No," Riley insisted. "It is the Comancheros you must destroy. Let me handle this."

Fargo looked closely at Riley. The madness appeared to have burned itself out, Riley's eyes revealing now only a cold, unbending resolve. "What've you got in mind, Riley?"

"When a fox approaches a prairie chicken's nest of young 'uns, she makes a big show, struts at bit, then runs off, taking the fox with her."

"What's that?" Charlie asked, looking up from his rifle. "You plannin' to make like a prairie chicken?"

But Fargo knew precisely what Riley meant. "Don't be a fool, Riley. Stay with us."

"No," said Riley.

As he spoke, he lifted his sorrel to a lope and a moment later broke from the timber and headed directly toward the lead Comanches. There were four of them riding in a close group, and when they saw Riley, they pulled up in some astonishment.

Dismounting swiftly and unlimbering their weapons, Fargo and the others crouched in the brush at the timber's edge and watched as Riley, brandishing his rifle, shouted something at the Comanches, then lifted his horse to a gallop, still heading straight for them.

By the time the astonished Comanches realized what Riley was about, it was too late. His rifle cracked and the lead redskin slipped from his horse. Still pounding toward them, Riley flung away his rifle, drew his Colt, and began firing rapidly. Two other Comanches toppled from their ponies before the outraged Indians broke into a headlong charge to meet him.

At once Riley cut his mount sharply to the right and galloped off, heading down the meadow—and away from Fargo and the others. The Comanche war party wheeled after him. Not long after, their war cries fading, they disappeared into the mists still hovering close over the meadowland.

"Mount up," Fargo called, reaching for his pinto's reins.

Charlie clambered up onto his wagon seat, Buffalo Wallow and the rest of the Indians flung themselves onto their horses, and together they charged out of the timber and across the meadowland until they had put the Comanche war party—and Mike Riley—far behind them.

8

They did not make camp until sundown. When they did, they chose a high meadow cut by a swift, ice-cold mountain stream. Everyone was exhausted, and soon after they had eaten, they put down their bedrolls and slept—but not without posting sentries and not without most of them selecting spots some distance from the campfire.

Fargo came awake suddenly, the feel of Charlie's hand on his shoulder.

"We got visitors," Charlie said.

Fargo flung aside his slicker and reached for his rifle. "Comanches?"

"No. Mexicans."

"How many?"

"Can't tell. One of the sentries thought he saw a couple slipping through the trees and woke me. I saw some more coming from the other side. We're surrounded."

"Did you wake the others?"

"Buffalo is seeing to it."

"What's the plan?"

"Buffalo said maybe we should lie low, wait until they make their move, then open up on them."

"Good idea." Fargo saw a clump of bushes a few feet above him on the slope. "We better get up there behind those bushes."

In a moment, wide awake, his Henry and his Sharps beside him, Fargo waited. It was not more than an hour before dawn. The moon was no longer overhead, but Fargo could still make out Charlie's wagon sitting alongside the stream, and he could see the dim shapes made up of blankets and saddles, the sleeping decoys the Indians had left. He had no idea where the Indians had slipped off to, though he was pretty certain some were hiding in the wagon while others were taking cover behind the stream's embankment.

"Our guests will probably make for that wagon first thing," Fargo muttered.

"Let them," Charlie said.

Bringing his Henry out in front of him, Fargo propped it up on a hillock and sighted on the wagon, then relaxed, waiting patiently. So long did he wait he was beginning to wonder if this wasn't going to turn into a false alarm, until he saw the first shadowy figure materialize out of the pines and, crouching, run swiftly down the slope to the meadow.

A moment later a second shadow slipped from the pines farther down, and then a third. From the size of their hats and the fact that most of them were wearing serapes, Fargo knew the report that they were Mexican was correct.

And Mexican in these parts usually meant Comancheros.

Then, less than twenty yards to the right of Fargo and Charlie, more Mexicans left the pines and moved swiftly across their field of vision, continuing on down the slope toward the wagon. They moved in a low crouch, their rifles held in readiness. In the moonlight, their white, loose-fitting pants contrasted sharply with the dark weave of their ponchos. A few had cartridge belts across their chests.

And they kept coming, sifting down out of the pines with a speed and swiftness that impressed Fargo.

"I count at least ten," Charlie whispered.

"More than that. Twelve."

As they spoke, Mexicans gained the meadow from a thick clump of pine on the slope directly across from them. Fargo picked out one of the Mexicans approaching the wagon, rested his sight on the fellow's cartridge belt, and waited. It would be fatal, he realized, to open up with the rest of the Mexicans still in the pines above them. He was sure Buffalo Wallow and the rest of the Utes realized this as well.

But Fargo did not find it easy to hold his fire. Not with them murdering bastards liable to open up on them at any moment.

Fargo heard a soft rustle behind him. Before he could turn, the cold touch of a revolver's muzzle was pressed gently but firmly aginst the back of his neck, close behind his left ear. At the same time Fargo heard Charlie's gasp.

"Stay, gringo," Fargo heard from behind him. "Do not move."

Fargo froze and waited. A rough, strong hand grabbed the back of his shirt and flung him around. Fargo found himself staring up at one of the Mexicans. The son of a bitch had a cocked Colt .44 in his hand, its muzzle yawning open a few inches from his nostrils. Out of the corner of his eyes, Fargo caught a glimpse of Charlie, face down in the grass, another Mexican leaning his knee on the small of the old man's back. Charlie was struggling feebly to free himself.

The Mexican behind the Colt smiled.

"Call off your dogs," he said, "or I'll blow your gringo brains all the way down this hill."

"I can't do that."

"What do you mean?"

"My men aren't where you think they are."

The Mexican cursed in Spanish and shouted a warning to the Mexicans converging on the wagon. At once his men turned, darted back across the meadow, heading up into the pines. Buffalo Wallow and the rest of the Indians opened up on them.

The Mexican standing over Fargo was dismayed. He lifted up to see more clearly what was happening below in the meadow and Fargo grabbed his Colt, then kicked his feet, catching the Mexican in his midsection. The Colt went off, the bullet plowing into the ground beside Fargo's head as Fargo thrust upward with his legs and dug his shoulder down into the ground. With a muffled cry the Mexican went flying over Fargo's head and down the slope.

The other Mexican lifted his knee off Charlie so he could turn his Colt on Fargo. Before he could do so, Charlie snatched up his rifle and clubbed the man on the side of his head. As he went stumbling backward, his Colt discharged harmlessly into the air. Charlie jumped on him. While the two men grappled, Fargo unsheathed his knife and flung himself down the slope after the stunned Mexican. The fellow was just pushing himself up off the ground when Fargo came down hard with both knees on the small of his back. Grabbing his hair, Fargo yanked the Mexican's head back, then pressed the blade of his bowie hard against his taut jugular.

"Call off your men, you bastard," Fargo told him.

"No can breathe," the man gasped.

Fargo let the man's head pull forward an inch or two, but kept the bowie's blade tight against his throat.

Bitterly, reluctantly, the Mexican leader cried out in Spanish to his men. Whatever he told them, the steady return fire from the pines quickly subsided. A moment later the gunfire from the wagon and the riverbank fell off also and a sudden, eerie silence fell over the meadow.

Slowly, carefully, Fargo hauled the Mexican leader to his feet. The man had lost his Colt when he tumbled down the slope. He patted him for a knife, found one in his belt and stuck it into his own belt, then yanked the man's arm around and twisted it up behind his back.

"March," Fargo ordered, pushing the fellow ahead of him down the steep slope toward the smoldering campfire.

When they reached it, Fargo told his prisoner to order his men to come down out of the pines.

The man did as he was bid. An anxious query came from somewhere in the pines off to their left, which the Mexican answered with authority. A moment later, his men began drifting cautiously down the slopes toward them. At that moment Charlie arrived with his prisoner, and a few seconds later Buffalo Wallow and the rest of the Indians emerged from the darkness around the wagon to stand with Fargo as the Mexicans approached.

"Anyone hurt?" Fargo asked Buffalo Wallow.

The big Indian shook his head. "These Comanchero bad shots."

"Good."

"We are not Comancheros," said the Mexican beside Fargo indignantly. "It is you who are Comancheros."

"You're crazy, mister," said Charlie.

"If you not Comancheros, what you do here?"

"Hell, that's just what we were going to ask you," said Fargo.

The conversation ended abruptly when the Mexicans, having reached to within fifty yards or so of the wagon, halted and refused to go a step farther.

"Tell them to drop their weapons," Fargo told the Mexican.

The Mexican laughed. "They will not do this."

"What do you mean?"

"It is good you do not understand Spanish. I have told them to come down, line up before you, and when I give the signal, begin shooting. It will be bloody, my friend, but it will satisfy my soul and those of my brothers to take you bastards to hell with me."

"Now hold it right there," said Fargo. "Don't you think we ought to talk about this?"

"Why talk, gringo? Are you afraid to die?"

"I'm not afraid to die; I'm just not anxious for it to happen."

The Mexican smiled. "I admit. What you say makes sense. So talk. Say what you wish."

"You said you aren't with the Comancheros. Well, dammit, neither are we! Maybe we ought to find out who the hell we are before we start blowing one another's asses into hell and gone." When Fargo finished his statement, he pulled the bowie away from the Mexican's throat and released him.

"I repeat what I say before," the Mexican said. "I am not Comanchero. Neither are my men."

"Then what in hell were you trying to do up there?"

"Kill Comancheros."

"Where you from?"

"Nogales."

"You're a long way from Mexico, aren't you? This here's Arizona Territory."

"Two months ago your leader, Fletcher, raided our people, plundered our ranches, raped our women and carried off our workers in the field. This was the second raid in a year. Our stupid government does nothing to punish them and the American government thinks only of their stupid war. We have had enough."

"So you've come all this way to take on Hawk Fletcher and his Comancheros."

"That is what I say," the Mexican repeated, no longer as belligerent, the first faint sign in his manner that he might indeed have been wrong in assuming Fargo and his people were Comancheros.

"Then tell your men to put down their guns. We're on our way to take Hawk Fletcher down a peg, too. Maybe we should join forces." As Fargo spoke, he sheathed his knife and stuck out his hand. Finding it a little difficult to believe, the Mexican frowned. Then he took Fargo's hand and shook it. Finding the Mexican's grip strong, Fargo pumped heartily and smiled.

At once the Mexican relaxed.

"My name is Skye Fargo," Fargo told him.

"And I am Alfonso de Carvajal."

"I'll just call you Al," said Charlie, stepping forward then to shake de Carvajal's hand.

That broke the last of the tension. The line of Mexicans facing them lowered their weapons and joined Fargo and the rest, and both sides spent the next ten or fifteen minutes getting acquainted and ascertaining what damage, if any, either force had inflicted on the other. It was found that one Mexican had a flesh wound in his thigh that was easily seen to, and a Ute had suffered a mild concussion when a rock ricocheted up and struck him on the side of the head.

That was the extent of the injuries, and on learning this, de Carvajal proclaimed it a miracle—and also a sign that the two forces were destined to move on the Comancheros together.

"Sure," said Fargo, grinning, "I'll go along with that. But we sure as hell better do better with Fletcher's men than we did with each other."

De Carvajal's eyebrows lifted in appreciation of Fargo's observation. It was indeed a sobering thought.

A day later, an hour or so before sundown, Fargo, Charlie, Buffalo Wallow, and de Carvajal were peering down at Hell Town.

A lazy stream looped around one end of the town, a single plank bridge offering passage over it. Fronting both sides of a broad main street, Fargo counted ten solidly constructed frame buildings, one of them larger than two combined. All but three of the buildings boasted traditional false fronts. One of them had a porch.

Scattered haphazardly along rutted alleys behind the frame buildings was a sad collection of tents and tar-paper shacks, the more solid among them constructed of mud and logs. Well away from the rest of the town, about ten adobe huts had been set up on a small rise. It was a smaller and much neater settlement, complete with its own plaza.

The town had none of the usual amenities of a settled, civilized community. There were no churches, no water tower, no streetlamps, and not a single telegraph line or well-traveled road leading to or from the place. Hell Town looked exactly like what it was in truth: a place that had grown up out of hard necessity, filling a need for men on the run, enabling them to find here a place where they could meet with their fellows, strike a deal, and relax—a town where a man could let off steam at the same time he was doing business with the devil.

Yet now that Fargo had finally reached Hell Town,

he was vaguely disappointed. He had expected something considerably more spectacular, he realized wryly, perhaps the sharp whiff of brimstone.

Charlie nudged him. "The place looks nearly deserted."

Fargo nodded. Considering its size, there were few horses moving in or out of the place and a decided scarcity of men and women on the streets.

"Looks like Hawk Fletcher and his Comancheros are off on a raid," Charlie commented, his voice betraying disappointment.

"That's what I was thinking."

"So what do we do now?"

"It might be a good idea if someone went down there to find out."

"You volunteerin'?" Charlie asked.

"Yes."

"So am I."

De Cavajal had been standing beside them, peering down at Hell Town, saying nothing. He spoke up. "I go too, *amigos*."

"All three of us?" asked Fargo.

De Carvajal nodded. "That's right. One man, he will have hard time not getting eaten alive. Hawk Fletcher must have left some men behind to watch out for strangers."

Fargo looked back down at the town. De Carvajal was right. "Come ahead, then."

"*Bueno*. When do we leave?"

"Now's as good a time as any."

Fargo advised Buffalo Wallow of his decision, while de Carvajal went off to speak to his men. Not long after, the three men gained the valley floor farther down, then rode back across the barren, mesquite-pocked flat toward the cluster of buildings and huts.

They had agreed on a simple story. The three of them were on the run, so they had come to see if they could join the Hawk's forces. They knew such a request had little chance of being honored, but at least it gave them an excuse for being there and for asking questions.

As they rode into Hell Town, they noted that the largest and most solidly built structure of all, the one diagonally across from the hotel, had few windows. Along one side of the building there was a loading platform with large gates behind it, spacious enough to allow passage of the sizable shipments of livestock and other goods. As he rode by, Fargo glimpsed extensive pens and corrals behind the building. Fargo realized that this was the Comancheros' commissary—the storehouse for their loot, gunpowder, weapons, ammunition, even their rustled livestock and horse-flesh.

The livery stable was next to the commissary. It was a huge barn with an oversized corral behind it. As the three men dismounted in front of it, the hostler, squinting in the sun, ducked out of the shadowed entrance, took their horses, and led them into the dim, cool interior.

What Fargo noted at once was the barn's enormous capacity—that, and the huge pile of horse manure in the alley beside the livery. This was a livery designed to handle at least fifty horses, yet all Fargo could see were empty stalls, all of which meant that a sizable force must have left Hell Town with Hawk Fletcher and was still on the trail somewhere, either going or coming back from whatever unhappy town the leader of the Comancheros had targeted.

Fargo flipped a coin at the hostler and the three left the livery and crossed the street to the saloon. It was the only building with a porch, and a sign nailed upon the porch roof proclaimed it a hotel as well. That made it convenient enough. The saloon was supplying its patrons with handy rooms to take their night's pick.

They peered over the batwings. The saloon was almost empty. The barkeep, a huge man with a shiny bald head and shoulders almost as broad as Fargo's, was poised expectantly behind the counter. He had obviously been waiting for them. As they pushed their way through the batwings, however, he looked quickly away and began polishing the bar.

They strolled up to the bar and Fargo shoved his hat back off his forehead. "Beer," he told the barkeep.

"We ain't got no beer."

"Whiskey, then."

The barkeep slapped a bottle down onto the bar and placed a shot glass before each man. Fargo poured his drink and passed the bottle to his companions, then looked around the saloon. Only three men were sitting at the tables, and in the back a quiet poker game was in progress. A faro table was sitting in a corner with a sheet over it.

"Quiet town," Fargo commented to the barkeep. "Where the hell is everybody? We expected some action. We rode a long ways."

The barkeep looked at Fargo for a long time, then turned his back on him and walked the length of the bar. Lifting the counter gate, he disappeared into a room. He slammed the door loudly behind him.

"Welcome to Hell Town," Fargo commented.

"You see the size of that stable out there?" Charlie asked.

"And the size of that manure pile in the alley?" de Carvajal reminded them as he sipped his drink. "The big man, he is away—and he has taken his army with him."

Fargo shook his head unhappily. "The bastard's on another shopping expedition."

The three men were quiet for a moment as they contemplated what that meant to the many innocents caught in Hawk Fletcher's wake.

"Let's sit down," Fargo suggested.

There were plenty of tables to choose from, so they selected one in the back along the far wall that gave them an unobstructed view of the batwings and the saloon's other occupants. The poker players never once looked up, and the remaining patrons shot back only cold stares whenever the three men glanced their way.

They were not exactly welcome.

Until it was completely dark, the three of them drank steadily, quietly. Then, the bottle emptied, they got to their feet and left the saloon, coming to an uncertain halt on the porch. The town was as dead as a Quaker meeting, and about as interesting. Fletcher was off looting somewhere and there was no hint of when he and his murderous band would be returning.

As they stood there, de Carvajal began studying the neat adobe huts on the rise outside of town. Abruptly, he lifted his sombrero off his head, then placed it back down at a slightly more rakish angle. "I think maybe I ride over to them adobe houses," he said. "Maybe I find some señorita who like to talk."

"I don't have any better ideas," said Fargo.

The two men watched the Mexican saunter back across the street to the livery and a moment later ride out, heading for the neat white squares sitting on the hill. As soon as he had vanished into the darkness, the batwings behind them opened. Fargo and Charlie turned.

Two girls were standing in the doorway. "Buck say you come long way for good time," the nearest girl said. Then she smiled brilliantly. "We don't think you should go away disappointed."

"Who the hell's Buck?" Fargo asked.

"The bartender."

Charlie chuckled. "That's what I'd call a real change of heart."

"Come back inside," said the other girl, a small, round woman with dancing eyes, as she reached up and took Charlie's arm. "You ain't afraid of me, are you?"

"Hell, no," Charlie responded eagerly, his old face turning crimson under his whiskers. He patted the girl's hand and winked at Fargo. "Ain't afraid of nothin' I can eat or play with."

Fargo and Charlie went back inside with the girls.

The poker game was still in progress, but the other three patrons were gone. The barkeep was back behind the bar. The girls guided them over to the door through which the barkeep had vanished, and showed them up a narrow flight of stairs that led to the upstairs hotel.

On the second-floor landing they found a small cubbyhole of a front desk and behind it a thin-faced weasel of a man.

"A room for the night, gents?"

Charlie nodded eagerly. The clerk handed them a quill pen. They signed and followed the girls down the narrow hallway to their rooms. Fargo entered his room first. Charlie, smiling foolishly at Fargo, kept on down the hallway and disappeared into the next room with his catch.

The prelimininaries were cut-and-dried. The girl closed the door, introduced herself as Jo Anne, and stepped out of her dress. She had a lank, pale body with sagging breasts and a scant pubic patch and wore no perfume or face paint. A faint musty odor pervaded her or the room, Fargo couldn't tell which. Without ceremony, she undressed Fargo with quick, casual fingers and pushed him gently back onto the bed and mounted him, kissing him once or twice on the lips.

Fargo was bored.

When she saw this, she pulled back, her eyes narrowed in suspicion. "What kind of excitement you want?" she asked. "You like boys?"

It was a meant as a taunt, Fargo realized, but he felt himself stiffen in surprise and anger at the coldness with which it was delivered. He almost struck her, but held himself back and managed a smile.

"No. It's not that. But I hardly know you."

"You want the story of my life. Is that it?"

"That's right. Tell me, what's a nice girl like you doing in a place like this?"

She looked at him coldly for a minute. "I'm fuckin' men who pay promptly. This is goin' to cost you two silver dollars. You got it?"

"Sure."

"Maybe you better put it on the dresser so I can see it."

Fargo got up, fished in his pants, produced the coins, and slapped them down on the top of the dresser. "Maybe," he suggested, "if we could have some drinks sent up."

"That's extra."

Fargo flipped her a coin. She had been sitting up on the edge of the bed, watching him carefully. Snatching the coin deftly out of the air, she stood up. It took only a second for her to pick up her dress, step into it, and vanish out the door. Fargo went to the window as soon as the door closed behind her and looked down at the street. Not a single horseman clopped by. The town appeared to be completely deserted. The only sign of life was the hostler sitting on a chair in front of his stable, a cigar in his mouth.

And a shotgun resting across his lap.

"Here we are," said the girl, entering the room and kicking the door shut behind her. She had two glasses in one hand, a bottle in the other. With the top of the dresser serving as a bar, she poured out two drinks.

117

"I hope this helps " she said, handing Fargo his.

"Yeah. Me too

"What's your name anyway?"

"My name's Fargo, Skye Fargo."

Sipping the raw whiskey, he went over to the window and glanced down. The hostler was still sitting in front of the livery stable with his shotgun, and now, farther up the street, in the shadow of a log shack, another man was standing, his horse behind him, something metallic gleaming in his right hand.

A few of the tents in the back streets glowed from the lamps inside, and only a few men or women were visible moving about the town. The sudden trill of a woman's laughter came from somewhere below; and closer to the hotel, Fargo heard the sharp sound of a bottle shattering. The town was not entirely dead, he realized, but it had a deadly air of waiting about it, as if a curtain were about to be raised and a grim play about to begin.

He put down his empty glass on the windowsill and, walking over to his gun belt, removed the Colt and placed it under his pillow.

Smiling at Jo Anne, he said, "Just a precaution."

"You gunsels are all alike," she said. "You think more of your six-guns than you do of a woman."

"There isn't that much difference," Fargo admitted. "They're both just as dangerous."

He sat down on the edge of the bed and pulled the girl down beside him. The town had seemed quiet, even harmless, but Fargo had just had a glimpse beneath the surface and knew the place was on the verge of exploding at any moment—with Fargo and

Charlie serving as the detonators. So it was about time, he figured, to find out what this hired woman was made of and what her role in all this would turn out to be.

Her whiskey breath helped him a little as she kissed him boldly, then pressed him down beneath her again. She appeared to be warming to her task, but Fargo was aware every minute that that was indeed what it was: a task, an assigned task.

Nevertheless, he found himself giving way to her insistent professionalism. When he was slow to gain an erection, her lips moved swiftly down his torso and soon coaxed his shaft back to life. Once he felt the urgency building within him, he rolled over onto her, his big hands lifting her buttocks and swinging them in under him. Then he drove down into her as deep and as hard as he could. She gasped in surprise, as if this was something she hadn't expected.

She spread her legs, lifted her thighs, and enclosed his waist with her legs, locking her ankles behind his back. He lifted forward and thrust almost straight down, powerfully slamming himself deep into her. Then he pulled almost all the way out and surged back down into her a second time, then another and another, building to a fury as he went deeper and deeper with each thrust. It was almost as if he were trying to punish her for something he felt she was about to do to him.

She began to cry out. He knew then she was no longer going through the motions. Her face twisted and her mouth opened, and he covered her lips with his. She bit at his lips, moving under him and seeming to flinch away and move toward him at the same time. The taste of her whiskey breath, the musky scent of her hair, and the feel of her suddenly alive body pulsing and arching under him intensified his desire into an all-consuming urge that transformed his suspicion and wariness into a brutal, overpowering urge to take her, to blow the top of her head off with the intensity of his lovemaking.

She seemed to sense this and he felt sudden, sharp pain as her fingernails dug into his shoulders. He increased his tempo and found himself looking down at her with a smile on his face. Seeing this, she gasped and stiffened. Then, panting shallowly, quickly, eagerly, she began shuddering violently under him. He could see she was no longer in control, that her orgasm had rushed upon her unaware, sweeping all her caution and cold professionalism away. Gasping with each pulse of her orgasm, she cried out, uttering tiny little sobs of pleasure.

That did it. He came then too, impaling her on the bed, pressing home as he pulsed once, twice, and still more—emptying himself completely into her. When at last he had nothing left, he slowly lifted off her, aware suddenly of how hard he was panting. She lay passive and unmoving under him, her legs resting flat on the bed, her thighs splayed apart.

"You son of a bitch," she muttered, a faint, pleased smile on her face, "it took you long enough to get going, but once you did . . ."

"Just don't like to see a woman fake it," he said, "or have to."

She chuckled. "You got a smoke on you?"

120

"No."

She rolled over, opened a drawer in the bedstand, and took out a pack of cheroots and some wooden matches. Sitting up with her back to the bed, she lit a cheroot for him and then one for herself.

"It's on the house," she said.

"Thanks."

"You three men are in trouble, you know."

"Why?"

"You ain't welcome. You rode into a bad place and you ain't goin' to ride out again."

"That so?"

"That's the way it is. I don't make the rules. I just work here. I do the best I can and keep my skirts clean. No one who goes against Hawk Fletcher lives to tell about it."

"Me and my friends just want to join up."

"Hawk don't take no volunteers. And he's got enough riders, Comancheros who been tradin' with the Comanches for two generations. It is a closed world, and you or no one else is going to break into it."

"We'll see about that. Once we get a chance to talk to Hawk, he might have a change of heart."

"I don't think so."

"When's he due back?"

"Any day now. Maybe tomorrow or the next day. But that don't matter one way or the other."

"Why not?"

"You'll be dead by then."

Fargo took his gun out from under the pillow, then got up and dressed, flipping the gun from one hand to the other and watching her all the while. "Mind if I ask you a question?" he asked, strapping his six-gun around his waist.

"Go ahead." The tip of her cheroot glowed as she inhaled deeply.

"What's your part in all this?"

"I'm supposed to keep you busy while the boys get things organized."

At that moment the door slammed open. Fargo turned to see two men, guns drawn, striding into the room. He drew his Colt, but as he brought it up, Jo Anne flung a pillow at him. It caught him in the face, blocking his view.

Ducking low, he dived for the window, the two men blasting away at him. The windowpane shattered as he lowered his head and slammed through the window's sash. He felt himself twist once in midair, then slam, faceup, onto the porch roof, the breath momentarily knocked out of him.

Above him one of the two men poked his head and shoulders out of the window, then aimed carefully down at Fargo. He took too long. Fargo fired up at him, sending two slugs into him—one catching his shoulder, the other his face. He sagged over the sill, blocking the window until someone pulled him back into the room.

By that time Fargo had rolled to the edge of the roof. He dropped to the ground just as the second man fired at him from the window. Starting across the street, Fargo whirled and flung a round up at him. The second gunman cried out and plunged forward out the window.

But Fargo was no longer interested in him. It was

the hostler's turn now as he raced across the wide street to intercept Fargo, his shotgun at the ready. Fargo flung himself to the ground, steadied his aim, and squeezed the trigger. The hostler went down as if someone had tripped him with a wire. Scrambling to his feet, Fargo holstered his six-gun, raced toward the downed hostler, and snatched up the man's shotgun. A second later he pounded into the livery stable.

A shadowy form loomed from a stall.

Fargo fired one barrel and blew the son of a bitch back into a pile of horse shit. The few horses inside the barn began whinnying frantically, but Fargo paid no attention as he pulled his pinto out of his stall and began saddling him. He was buckling the cinch strap when running feet just outside the livery entrance caused him to raise the shotgun.

One of Fletcher's gunmen appeared in the barn doorway, his six-gun out. He was confused. Leaning forward and shading his eyes, he cried, "Seth! You in there? The son of a bitch got away."

Fargo answered him with another blast from the hostler's shotgun. The fellow buckled and vanished from sight—as if a wind had taken him.

Flinging away the shotgun, Fargo reloaded his Colt and checked to make sure his Henry was still in his saddle scabbard. It was. He had left the Sharps up on the ridge, in Buffalo Wallow's care. It would be the Indian's if Fargo did not slip out of this particular noose.

Mounting up, he spurred his pinto and, head down, clattered out of the barn, then pulled up in the middle of the street. No one fired at him. They were waiting for his next move. But first Fargo had to know if Charlie was still back in the hotel—and still alive.

Looking up at the hotel, Fargo cried, "Charlie, get on down here."

There was a faint woman's scream and then the sound of a window shattering. A second later Charlie thrust his bearded head out.

"Go on," he cried. "I've got more'n I can handle here! Get out while you can."

Before Charlie could say anything more, rough hands yanked him back into the room. Fargo wheeled his pony then and trotted down the street—only to see four horsemen approaching to meet him. They were riding abreast, rifles resting across their saddle horns. They appeared to be in no hurry at all.

Fargo leaned suddenly forward and spurred toward them. In reply, they lifted their horses to a lope and spread out farther. Hauling up his six-gun, Fargo waited until he got closer. The riders brought up their rifles.

Abruptly, from out of the shadows beside them, de Carvajal charged into the four riders, firing as he came. The sudden, unexpected assault completely demoralized the four riders. They began milling in a desperate attempt to protect their flanks, but before they could do so, one, then two riders were shot from their saddles.

Fargo was in their midst by this time, and when one of the horsemen tired to break away, Fargo spurred after him. The rider turned his horse sharply, desperate to escape. Fargo sent two quick shots after him. As the horse disappeared into the night, the rider slipped from his back.

Charging back to the milling horses and downed riders, Fargo found that de Carvajal had dealt with the remaining gunman. The two men wheeled their horses and headed back the way they had come, not a single shot fired after them. Fargo should have been jubilant, considering his good fortune in having escaped from almost certain capture, if it were not for the fact that Charlie Kettle was now a prisoner in Hell Town.

9

Once they reached the camp, Fargo found that de Carvajal's news was good.

As de Carvajal had surmised, the adobe settlement on the rise had been built for the Comancheros' women and it had not been difficult for him to find one señorita who was still more than a little upset with her abduction three years earlier and her forced alliance with one of the Comancheros. With de Carvajal's arms around her and his gentle lips on hers, she had willingly told him all they needed to know.

The day before, a scout had arrived to tell the town that Hawk Fletcher and his Comancheros would arrive soon. They had plundered a Texas town near the Gulf and were returning with wagonloads of booty, and word was already being sent to the Comanches to tell them of the fine rifles that could now be obtained through trade or purchase. Soon—as custom dictated—there would be a ripsnorting, double-barreled celebration to welcome Fletcher's return.

Late the next afternoon, just as de Carvajal's lady friend had told him they would, the Comancheros arrived, the dust from their many, heavily laden wagons hanging in the air long after they rolled into Hell Town. By nightfall the celebration was in full swing.

That same night Fargo was standing with de Carvajal and Buffalo Wallow, peering down at Hell Town, noting the growing uproar with some satisfaction. Hawk Fletcher and his Comancheros obviously believed they were now perfectly safe from their enemies. It had not occurred to Fletcher that any of those he had plundered would follow him this deep into the Sawtooths.

De Carvajal chuckled. "That place down there, it will be in one uproar soon, *amigo*," he remarked to Fargo. "The whiskey will turn them all mad. Then we will send down upon them the vengeance of God."

De Carvajal was referring to a scheme Fargo had already set in motion.

Since Hell Town was almost directly under them—the sheer slopes too steep for either horses or men to climb or descend—what Fargo had in mind was bombarding Hell Town from above. The missiles—most of which had already been constructed—were nothing more than large balls of brush lashed together and filled with dry grass, then doused with the kerosene Fargo had taken from the company store. Set afire and sent bounding down the steep slope, they would rain upon the buildings and tents of Hell Town, setting fires everywhere.

Fargo had already impressed upon everyone the importance of certain targets, the huge commissary building across from the hotel, especially. It would most likely be packed from floor to ceiling with the gunpowder and ammunition the Comancheros had just brought back. Then, with the town in flames, de Carvajal and Buffalo Wallow's forces would sweep in and cut down the Comancheros that remained—including the big man, Hawk Fletcher.

It was a neat-enough plan, and Fargo couldn't see any holes in it. But he had been mulling things over and had come to a decision. The attack on Hell Town would just have to wait. Charlie Kettle was still down there somewhere, and if he was still alive, they would have to get him out before they sent those flaming bushes down the slope.

Fargo looked at de Carvajal. "That vengeance of God is going to have to wait some."

"Why is that, *amigo*?"

"We can't move on them until Charlie's safely out of there."

De Carvajal considered that fact for a moment, then shrugged. "But of course, señor. If that is what you wish. But tell me, how do you plan to get him out?"

"I figure I'll wait till the whiskey and the women really take hold down there—then go and get him. It shouldn't be all that difficult."

"I go with you," said Buffalo Wallow.

"No, Buffalo. I'd better go alone. It'll be easier for one man to sneak in and join their party."

The big Indian was not happy at this, but he accepted Fargo's view of the matter. Fargo looked back at de Carvajal. "So it lookes like you and Buffalo Wallow will be in charge up here."

"We'll know what to do, *amigo*."

By nightfall, the tents were doing a fine business; there were bonfires throughout the town; and short-skirted women could be seen darting through the alleys and down the streets with men after them, their delighted laughter and occasional whoops coming clearly to those watching on the ridge. Early on in the celebration a single horseman had started galloping up and down main street, puncturing the night with gunfire until he fell or was shot out of his saddle. There were no more horsemen, but occasional gun-fire could be heard popping in the night.

A little before midnight, Fargo rode down to the valley, taking with him an extra mount for Charlie. Leaving the two horses in a clump of aspen near the foothills, Fargo continued on foot to Hell Town, coming in from the backside.

Stepping over a drunk lying facedown in his own vomit, he pushed open the saloon's back door and entered. The smoke in the long room was so thick Fargo could barely see as far as the wall. Blinking to keep his eyes from burning out, he found a chair in a corner and leaned back in it. Out of the smoke came a bucktoothed girl of thirteen or fourteen. She was a white girl, close to exhaustion. From the look of her dress and the bruise under her left eye, it was clear she had been used roughly this night. She tried to smile, but it had long since worn out.

"Sorry we ain't got no table, mister," she said, trying to brush back her untidy hair. "Can I get you anything?"

"A whiskey."

She nodded and vanished in the direction of the bar. Fargo looked about. Men were crowded two deep around tables, some playing cards, others faro, all of them drinking. Most of the men had women beside them, and whenever the women tried to pull back or see to other customers, they would be wrenched back cruelly. In the short time it took for the girl to bring Fargo his drink, two fights broke out. One of them ended in gunfire. It was over in seconds and the loser was dragged feetfirst from the saloon and dumped off the porch. The incident had no effect whatever on the two poker games in progress less than a few feet from the shooting.

These, then, were the ill-famed Comancheros, rough, brutal, loud, and as quick to kill as to laugh.

The girl returned with his whiskey. Fargo drank it greedily, gave the girl a coin, and sent her back for another. When she returned with it, he got to his feet and asked her to go outside with him. Fear, naked and abject, came into her eyes. He saw her shoulders sag in despair. She wanted to refuse, but didn't dare.

Smiling to allay her fears, Fargo said, "You don't have to worry none about me, young lady. It is grown woman, I prefer. I just need your help— some information."

This didn't help her much. Her fear still dominated her, but she shrugged resignedly and left the saloon with him, going out the back door. Drawing her away from the building—and from the privy's stench—he flung the empty glass into a bush and sat down on a low pile of firewood, patting a spot beside him.

Again the girl hesitated.

Fargo told her, "I just need your help. But if anyone comes out here and sees us, it's got to look like we're at least friendly."

Reluctantly, she sat down beside him. "My name's Amy," she told him in a small, scared voice.

"Where you from?"

"Presidio, Texas."

"Fletcher's Comancheros captured you?"

"Yes."

"When?"

"A year ago."

"Well, maybe this is the last day of your exile. How'd you like that?"

"You must be crazy, mister. No one can stop Hawk Fletcher."

"We'll see. Now, listen. I'm looking for an old man. He was captured here yesterday by Fletcher's men. The last time I saw him he was upstairs in a bedroom, with one of the girls works the saloon."

"Jo Anne?" Amy asked.

"No. Her friend. Jo Anne was with me."

"So you're the one."

"What do you mean?"

"Jo Anne's in real trouble 'cause you got away. They said she liked you so much, she warned you."

131

"She didn't warn me. Hell, I figured she was looking forward to seeing me get it. What've they done to her?"

"She got beat."

"How bad?"

"Bad enough so she ain't workin' the saloon tonight."

"Do you know where that old man is?"

"I saw them taking him to the back room." She turned and pointed to the second floor. There was a room in back with no lights on. Outside covered stairs led up to it.

"You say he's in there?"

"I don't know for sure if he's there now. Last time I knew for sure I could hear him screamin'. They was working him over pretty good."

Fargo swore softly, bitterly. He had been afraid of that. Nevertheless, he was certain Charlie had not told the men of Fargo's force waiting up there on the ridge. But what Fargo wasn't certain of was how he was going to be able to get Charlie out of here. From the sound of it, Charlie would most likely be in very bad condition.

As he pondered this, he glanced up at the mountain ledge towering high above the town. All day they had worked at the task of tying together the brush and grass. Now they were peering down, waiting. All he had to do was set fire to one of the three outhouses in back of these buildings. As soon as he did that, the flaming brush would be sent on its way.

Fargo looked back at Amy. "You better get back in there. And thanks. I hope you get out of this."

She started to leave him, then halted and turned back to face him. Something in his voice had warned her. "Why, mister? Why'd you say that?"

Fargo didn't want to tell her what was coming. On the other hand, he didn't want her to die in the flaming holocaust he knew would soon be raining down upon this town. "All I can say, Amy, is stay ready."

"Ready for what?"

"To run."

As she turned away again, a swarthy figure loomed out of the darkness and grabbed her arm. She yelped in sudden pain, sounding like a terrified puppy. Fargo's right fist closed over a fistful of sand as he got to his feet.

"Leave her be," he told the stranger.

The man hauled Amy roughly back to where Fargo was standing, his big Colt aimed at Fargo's chest. He was part Indian, with eyes of obsidian and hair as black as a crow's wing. Yet his features were pure Caucasian. It was a mean combination.

"I see you come in, mister," the breed said. "You don't belong with us. You try to hide in the smoke. Then you take this little one outside. I watch. You not even put your hands on her. It ain't her you want, it's what she knows."

"Who're you?"

"I am Silverado. Clay Silverado. I am second only to Hawk Fletcher. I think maybe I take you to him."

"Later. I'll see Fletcher later. I got other business first."

Silverado's eyes narrowed. "What other business is this?"

"The old man. The one they captured yesterday."

Silverado glanced briefly up at the room Amy had pointed out. That was all the confirmation Fargo needed. He flung his fistful of sand into Silverado's eyes. Dropping his gun, Silverado cried out as the sand struck his wide-open eyes and dug in under his eyelids. Collapsing to his knees, he blinked wildly and gouged at his eyes in a futile attempt to clean them, inadvertently driving the tiny grains of sand still deeper into his eye sockets.

Fargo kicked him in the head. As the man flipped over onto his back, unconscious, Fargo took Silverado's gun and stuck it into his belt. Fargo took the man's knife also. Then he looked over at Amy.

"Get back inside the saloon. If I were you, I'd say nothing about this to anyone."

"Si, señor," she said, reverting to Spanish in her awe at what Fargo had just done. "I go now. I tell no one!"

He watched her duck around the privy, and a second later the back door to the saloon opened and closed behind her. Fargo grabbed Silverado and flung him over his shoulder, then carried him to the outhouse. Pulling open the privy door, Fargo saw a man sleeping on the floor. Fargo stepped over him and flung Silverado facedown through one of the holes.

The Mexican sleeping on the floor stirred only slightly as Fargo closed the privy door behind him.

He hurried over the back steps leading to the second floor and took them two at a time. At the second-floor landing, he found a door and opened it and stepped inside. He was in the second-floor hallway of the hotel. There was a door to his right. Trying the knob, he found it was locked. He was about to shoot off the lock when he heard soft, stealthy movement on the other side of the door. He held up.

"Who's out there?" came a surly, unhappy voice.

"Silverado sent me," Fargo said. "He wants to see the old man."

"Who says so?"

"Hell, Silverado thought you'd be pleased. You want to stay in there with him all night?"

"Hell no!"

Fargo heard a key rattle in the lock. He stepped close just as the door was pulled open, and thrust the muzzle of his Colt into the guard's face. Rushing into the room, he slammed the man back against the wall and shifted the Colt so its muzzle was digging into the man's Adam's Apple.

"Charlie!" Fargo snapped over his shoulder. "You able to get up?"

There was an angry, muffled cry from the bed behind Fargo. Fargo raised his Colt swiftly and brought it down sharply on the man's head. The guard sank the length of the wall and uttered a wheezing sigh as he settled forward onto the floor.

Fargo spun about. His eyes were adjusted to the darkness now and he could see Charlie on the bed, a gag tied around his mouth, his wrists and ankles bound securely. There were raw welts on the old man's bare chest, and his left eye had swollen shut. It was not pleasant for Fargo to contemplate his friend as he untied first the gag and then cut through the rope binding his wrists and ankles.

Fargo lit a lantern, then pulled the old man to a sitting position. "You don't look so good," Fargo told him.

"I lost some teeth," the old man mourned unhappily. "That's the worst part. I didn't have all that many to begin with."

"Can you walk?"

"I got the pins and needles now, but give me a couple of minutes."

Fargo closed the door, examined the unconscious guard to make sure he was still out, then returned to the bed.

"Can you stand now?" he asked Charlie.

Slowly, carefully, Charlie heaved himself onto his feet. He teetered for a moment, but grabbing Fargo's shoulder, he managed to remain upright. Then he took a careful step forward, and then another.

"By grannies, it's goin' away," he said. "I'll be able to walk in a jiffy."

"Good. I got a horse waiting for you."

"You're a damn fool for comin' after me like this. But I sure do 'preciate it."

"Did you see Hawk Fletcher?"

"I did. He was curious about me. He's a tall feller with black eyebrows and black hair and eyes like bottomless pools. He's as tall as you, and maybe as strong. There's the whiff of damnation about him. He's a fellow stepped out of hell, Fargo."

"So maybe that's where we'll send him."

A knock came on the door. Both men spun to stare at it. The knock came again as Fargo strode swiftly to the door and took a position to one side of it.

"Hey, Jed," came a drunken call from the hallway. "Wake up!"

Whoever it was, he wanted the guard, not Charlie.

Holding his hand over his mouth, Fargo called, "Whatta you want?"

"Hey, buddy! I got you some company. The Hawk says you shouldn't have to suffer up here alone."

"That's right decent of him."

Fargo pulled open the door. A man of medium height, his back to Fargo, his spurs chinking heavily, clomped into the room dragging a girl behind him. The girl was Amy. When she saw Fargo, her eyes bugged, but he put his finger to his lips and slammed the door shut behind them.

The Comanchero spun around, blinking in confusion. "Hey! You ain't Jed!"

"That's right," said Fargo, leaning forward and slipping the man's Colt from his holster and cocking it.

"Son of a bitch! Who *are* you?"

"A friend of that old-timer you been beating on. Now, get over to the wall there, alongside Jed."

"What're you gonna do?" the fellow sputtered.

"This," Fargo said, clubbing the man on the forehead.

He slammed back against the wall, and a moment later was crumpled unconscious over the body of his friend.

Fargo turned to Amy. "We meet again."

"Yes."

"Go on back downstairs. Sneak out of this place. Then run and keep running."

"Why?"

"Never mind. Just do it."

A sharp, commanding voice came from the still-open doorway. "Now why should Amy do that, mister?"

Fargo spun to see the man Charlie had just described—Hawk Fletcher—stride into the room, a pearl-handled revolver gleaming in his right hand, a grin on his dark face.

Fargo looked down at Amy. "You told him. Why?"

"I was scared," she said, tears crowding the corners of her eyes. "I don't want no trouble."

"Go on back downstairs," Hawk Fletcher told Amy. "You did fine. You ain't got nothing more to worry about."

As Amy darted fearfully from the room, Hawk Fletcher turned to Fargo. "You came back here to rescue this old fossil, did you?"

"I did."

"He says you and him want to join us. I could not get him to shake that story. And he wouldn't tell me your name. Who are you?"

"Skye Fargo."

"I don't know you, do I?"

"I don't think we ever laid eyes on each other before."

Fletcher shrugged. "It's a shame to waste such gallantry, but we don't need more men, especially gringos—and it is my policy never to let snoopers like you and that old wreck go free once I catch them, a rule I have never broken."

As he spoke, three other men rushed past him into

the room and promptly disarmed Fargo. One of them was startled to find in Fargo's possession the gun and knife Fargo had taken from Silverado. He handed them to Fletcher.

Frowning, Fletcher held the weapons out to Fargo. "These belong to one of my lieutenants, Silverado."

"That's right."

"You took them from the breed? I do not believe it."

Fargo shrugged. "Believe what you want."

"You killed him?"

Fargo shrugged. "I'm not sure."

"Where is he?"

Fargo went to the window, lifted the sash, and pointed down at the privy. "He's in that privy—up to his armpits in shit."

"You crazy bastard," Fletcher cried, elbowing past Fargo and staring down at the privy.

Pulling himself back into the room, Hawk Fletcher turned to his men and began issuing orders rapidly in Spanish.

As Fletcher watched them charge out of the room, Fargo snatched up the lantern and slammed Fletcher back out of his way. Before Fletcher could recover, Fargo leaned out the window and flung the lantern. It struck the privy's roof and burst into flames.

Fargo swung back into the room just as Fletcher was hauling up his weapon to blast Fargo. Before he could, Charlie grabbed him from behind. The gun went off harmlessly, punching a hole in the ceiling. As the two men grappled for the weapon, Fargo stepped close, grabbed Fletcher by the shoulder, spun him around, and caught him as hard as he could with a right cross to the jaw.

The blow knocked Fletcher back, but he shook off its effects and, still groggy, went for Fargo. Fargo stepped in closer, and before Fletcher could raise his guard, he jabbed the man in the midsection, then came around again with a measured, sledging blow to the tip of Fletcher's chin. The man's head snapped around and his face went slack. Charlie stepped back to let Fletcher crumple to the floor.

The other two Fargo had dealt with earlier remained sprawled where he had left them, too groggy to stop Fargo or Charlie as they slapped on their hats, gathered up their weapons, and fled the room. As they headed down the hallway to the front stairs, they heard heavy footsteps tramping up the stairs from the saloon below.

There was a room to Fargo's right. He tried the doorknob. The room was locked. He lowered his shoulder and burst through. As the door slammed open, he dragged Charlie in after him and pushed the door shut. The two men they had heard coming up the stairs hurried past the door and on down the hall, one of them shouting to someone about a fire.

"That you, Fargo?"

It was a woman's voice. Fargo turned. In the dim light, he saw Jo Anne sitting up in her bed, a small derringer in her right hand, a grim cast to her face.

"That's right," he said.

"Good. I been waiting for a chance to blow you to hell, you miserable son of a bitch."

"Hold on a second."

"Why the hell should I?"

"Come to the window and I'll show you."

"I can't move. I been beat so hard I can hardly handle this gun."

"Then sit there and watch."

"Watch what? You some kind of a nut?"

During this conversation, Charlie had worked his way around to the other side of her bed. At Fargo's high sign, Charlie leapt for the girl. At the same time Fargo ducked. Jo Anne's gun went off, shattering the window, but Charlie had little difficulty twisting the gun out of her hand. She began to scream. Charlie clapped his hand over her mouth. Despite her supposed injuries, she continued to struggle furiously. Fargo was forced to lend his weight to Charlie's in order to keep the girl subdued and quiet.

A second later, more footsteps charged down the hallway. Men began shouting to one another from the ends of the hallway. Someone halfway up the stairs yelled something about the saloon porch, then turned and thumped back down again. A moment later they heard pounding footsteps coming from the room where Fargo had left Hawk Fletcher. As the footsteps came closer, Fargo could hear clearly Hawk Fletcher's angry voice.

Just before the men reached Jo Anne's room, she yanked her mouth free of Charlie's hand and opened it to cry out. Before she could, Fargo caught her on the chin with a short, brutal jab that knocked her senseless. Then he drew his gun and turned to face the door. But Fletcher and his men continued on past it down the stairs. As the sound of their feet faded,

Fargo became aware of a sudden, crackling sound and the strong whiff of smoke—this together with a growing escalation of cries and shouting from the street below.

"My God, what's that?" Charlie cried as a whirling fist of fire flashed past the window.

The bombardment has begun!

Fargo rushed over to look out, Charlie joining him.

The night had come alive with bounding, searing balls of fire that flung shards of flame in all directions as they careened past their field of vision. Long trailers of burning debris littered the street, and directly across from them, the livery stable was on fire, while the hostler and others were leading the terrified animals from the barn. As soon as they reached the street, many of the panicked horses broke loose from their handlers and raced off into the night.

Fargo glanced over at the commissary. So far, it remained untouched. But Fargo was satisfied that it would only be a matter of minutes before the flames from the stable spread to it also.

Farther down the street, a burning ball had wedged itself in an alley between two buildings. Both were now ablaze. In the distance, some tents and shacks were going up as well, while in the street below the window, the shouts of terrified men and women were reaching a crescendo as they ran about like ants fleeing a stomped nest. No one had yet tried to organize a bucket brigade, nor was anyone attempting to put out any fires. They raged unchecked, uncontrolled, spreading with frightening rapidity.

More flaming balls bounded into the street. A

horseman suddenly reversed his course in an attempt to outrun one of them. But the flaming missile overtook him, and he and the horse went down under its onslaught, the ball skittered wildly about, scattering flaming embers in every direction.

Standing beside Fargo, Charlie gasped. "Fargo, what the hell is going on here?"

"I'll explain later."

Fargo hurried to the bed and slung the still-unconscious Jo Anne over his shoulder. Waiting for Charlie to open the door for him, he hurried past him out of the room and headed down the stairs. As he and Charlie pushed through the door and stepped into the saloon, they found it already ablaze.

One of the flaming balls must have landed on or under the porch. It was now completely gone and the front of the saloon was a mass of flame. Caught in the doorway were the charred bodies of those who had attempted to crowd out of the saloon.

Pulling up, Fargo and Charlie crouched beside the bar, wincing from the shriveling heat. Windows in the saloon continued to crack and shatter, and Fargo could smell the kerosene that had been poured over the grass and bushes. Abruptly, another ball bounded against the flaming saloon front, lodging in the opening where the batwings had been. So hot were the flames where it had landed, the ball of fire exploded almost immediately, sending flaming shards into the saloon. Small fires sprang up everywhere.

"Out the back way," Fargo shouted, hefting Jo Anne onto his right shoulder. Bursting out of the saloon, they had to shield their faces from the still-blazing privy, but once past this threat, they found the back alley reasonably free of flames, though the smoke that now hung over the town was so thick it was difficult for Fargo to see very far ahead of him.

As they stumbled through the night, they found themselves keeping pace with Comancheros, hangers-on, and prostitutes who never gave them a second glance. Caught up in the horror of this night, no one had time to look closely at anyone else. At this moment they were all the same: terrified living creatures fleeing an awesome conflagration.

Veering down an alley to keep shy of a couple of blazing shacks, Fargo and Charlie—Jo Anne still slung over Fargo's back—ran out into the main street just as a portion of the commissary's roof collapsed. A second later the building was torn apart by a great explosion, the power of it such that Fargo and Charlie were knocked forward onto their knees, with Fargo unable to prevent Jo Anne from striking the ground hard.

The blow aroused her from her stupor. She opened her eyes. But as soon as she caught sight of the raging fires all around her, she went into a blind panic. Lashing out at Fargo, she managed to pull free of him. Before he could catch her, she was running wildly across the street, heading for what appeared to be the only building still unscathed.

Fargo wanted to go after her, but he was suddenly too busy as two flaming balls of grass and brush swept down on him and Charlie. Charlie managed to scramble out of the way of the first one, but the second one came at Fargo too fast, and all he could do was lay flat and let the fiery projectile skip over his back and keep going. Immediately Charlie was beside Fargo slapping out the flames with his hat.

A moment later they were up on their feet, running as hard as all the rest until they disappeared into the night.

Their horses were waiting where Fargo had left them. Mounting up, they galloped farther down the valley to meet de Carvajal and Buffalo Wallow's forces, which Fargo reckoned should have reached the valley by this time.

Before long, the two men saw a long line of horsemen charging out of the darkness ahead of them. Fargo and Charlie slowed up. The oncoming riders, having caught sight of them, spurred directly toward them. Pulling to a halt, Fargo realized that in the darkness there was no way the oncoming riders could be sure who they were.

"Raise your hands, Charlie," Fargo cried. "Quick!"

Charlie didn't have to be told twice, and both men waited with their hands in the air as the Utes and Mexicans quickly encircled them. Then Fargo heard de Carvajal's shout and a moment later, de Carvajal and Buffalo Wallow has pushed themselves through the crush of encircling horsemen. Pulling up alongside them, de Carvajal reached over and slapped Charlie heartily on the back.

"I'm glad to see you alive, *amigo*," he cried. "When I see all that fire down there, I think maybe now you beef roast."

Buffalo Wallow, too, was pleased. He managed to rearrange the lines in his face so as to resemble a smile as he sat back in his saddle and gazed at Charlie, his black eyes gleaming with pleasure.

"Old man," he said to Charlie, "you don't look so good in the face, but it is good you back. How you feel?"

"Ready to ride!"

"Good. We fight now!"

Wheeling their mounts, Fargo and Charlie joined the rest as they lifted their horses to a hard gallop and continued on to Hell Town.

10

The towering conflagration had turned night into day as Fargo and the others rode into the outskirts of Hell Town.

For a moment it appeared they were not going to find anyone to fight. Then about twenty mounted Comancheros cut through the smoke and flames to meet them. Six-guns and rifles filled the inferno-like night with gunfire. Riders on both sides were sent spilling from their saddles. Riderless horses reared, terrified, and galloped off. Inside of ten minutes the battle was over, with no more than five or six Comancheros managing to break through and vanish into the night.

As Fargo, de Carvajal and Buffalo Wallow pulled up to the take stock, Fargo glanced past the still-smoldering buildings at a long red line, the expanding border of a grass fire that had started well behind the buildings and was now eating its way toward the steep mountain slopes, leaving a black, smoking carpet in its wake. Closer at hand, a few cabins and buildings were still blazing, but most had collapsed in on themselves, leaving only great piles of smoldering ashes that glowed in the darkness like swarming eyes.

Then he glanced over at the bridge. Around it clustered what was most likely the surviving female population of Hell Town. The bridge and stream must have offered some protection from the searing heat as well as the blazing embers that had been raining down everywhere. He thought of Jo Anne then and wondered if she had made it to the stream. He doubted it. The last he had seen of her, she was in no condition to think that clearly.

Fargo glanced at de Carvajal. "What were your losses?"

"Few. Very few. Two, maybe three men. It is a great victory."

Suddenly de Carvajal caught sight of what could have been Comancheros riding hard for the adobe huts on the hill. At once, he waved his men together and galloped after them.

Watching them go, Buffalo Wallow nodded in understanding and turned to Fargo. "He remember woman he meet before. Now he save her—and maybe get more Comancheros too."

"You lose many men?" Charlie asked him.

"Four braves. But they take many Comancheros with them. It was good fight."

"It was a good fight, all right. But we didn't get them all. The rest could still be hiding in the brush or in those few buildings still standing."

Charlie nodded solemnly. "We'll just have to comb this town real careful tomorrow. Like a dog nippin' at fleas."

Buffalo Wallow was staring intently at the women huddled about the bridge. Noticing this, Fargo moved his pinto closer to the big Indian.

"What do you see that I don't, Buffalo?"

Buffalo Wallow's eyes grew darker. "Maybe some Comancheros hide behind women's skirts."

Fargo sat up straighter in his saddle and peered with renewed interest at the women clinging to the bridge like a flock of terrified chickens. Many of them were still dressed in their bright costumes and dresses. This night could not have been a pleasant one for any of them.

For that reason Fargo had been unwilling to disturb them. Now he studied them closer. Though they were still apparently upset and near panic, they were careful to keep close together so as to present to Fargo and his riders a solid, unbroken front. And a watchful few were keeping their eyes on Fargo and his companions.

Buffalo Wallow turned to his warriors. They, too, had been staring at the women.

"Let's take a closer look, Buffalo," Fargo said.

The big Indian motioned the Utes across the flat toward the bridge, Fargo joining them. When the women saw the Indians moving on them, their nervousness increased. A wail of terror broke from one woman. A few began easing back into the stream, groping for cover under the plank bridge.

"We're not going to hurt you," Fargo called out to them.

This seemed to give them no comfort. The milling about and the wailing increased. "You better not lay a hand on us," one older woman cried.

"She not need to worry," said Buffalo Wallow, his voice close to a chuckle. "She look like male elk."

They were within a stone's throw when one of the women was flung brutally down and two Comancheros stepped out of their midst and opened fire. At once the riders scattered, Fargo and Charlie racing for the bridge. Clattering over it, they wheeled and came at the stream from the other side. By then, the Utes had finished one of them, and the other was fleeing along the streambank.

Turning his pinto, Fargo closed behind him in a matter of seconds. Still running flat out, the Comanchero turned and fired up at Fargo, then bolted for a clump of aspen. Fargo kept after him and fired back. The fellow went down hard, vanishing in the tall grass, but that was no assurance he had been hit. Fargo leapt from his pinto and went after him.

Behind him, Charlie reined in his mount. "Careful, Fargo!"

Fargo caught movement less than five feet to his right and fired in that direction. The Comanchero went up on one knee and returned the fire. As the round sang past Fargo's cheek, Fargo fired back.

The hammer came down on an empty chamber.

With an oath, Fargo holstered his Colt and drew his bowie. The wounded man was frantically trying to scramble away through the thick grass. Fargo took after him, dived for him, coming down close enough to wrap one arm around him to slow him down. A moment later he was astride the man's back, his left arm tightening like a vise around his throat.

But the stench that assailed Fargo's nostrils caused him to retch, and for a moment he almost released the man. Instead, he plunged home his blade, burying it up to its hilt in the man's back.

Then Fargo stood up quickly and kicked the man over so he could see his face. All Fargo had was moonlight to see by; but it was enough for him to recognize the half-breed Silverado. Hawk Fletcher's lieutenant had somehow managed to escape that blazing privy and the foul, soul-shriveling stew into which he had been plunged.

Flinging off his clothes, Fargo plunged into the icy stream and began scrubbing his clothes and himself. It would be a long, cold night, but there was nothing on earth to equal the stench of aged human night soil.

Perhaps in killing Silverado, he had done the breed a favor.

Day brought a clearer picture of what they had accomplished, and to Fargo the melancholy realization that his quest had ended in failure.

Only one building remained standing, and that one had its insides completely razed. The other buildings, including most of the tents and shacks, were black, smoldering ruins with only thin traces of smoke still lifting from them. The commissary had been completely gutted, and all that could be salvaged from the wreckage were the bullets that had been blown out of their boxes and landed intact on the ground. A few handguns and rifles had also been blown free, and these too were salvageable. But little else had survived.

In the livery they found the carcasses of seven horses. But this was all that had been caught by the flames. The rest had escaped or been ridden off by the escaping Comancheros.

And one of those Comancheros was their leader, Hawk Fletcher.

"There ain't no reason for you to blame yourself," Charlie maintained. "Look what you did to Hawk Fletcher's hideout. Hell, these here Comancheros are sittin' dead in the water now. They ain't got no base and most of their manpower is gone."

"That's right, *amigo*," said de Carvajal. "They are finish now."

Fargo shook his head firmly. "Not while Hawk Fletcher is alive and well."

The men standing around Fargo's horse shrugged. They had tried. But it was obvious there was no chance of convincing Fargo that he had completed his mission. He knew only too well that he had accomplished nothing that was lasting. They had stomped the ants' nest, he had tried to point out to them, but the queen ant had gotten away and would soon be setting up another anthill someplace else.

Besides, he had made a promise to Conchita—and that he had failed to keep.

Buffalo Wallow stepped back from Fargo's horse.

"Go with the Great Spirit," he told Fargo. "My people will remember you."

"Thanks, Buffalo."

Resignedly, Charlie Kettle and Alfonso de Carvajal reached up in turn to shake Fargo's hand.

"You sure you won't come back with me, Charlie?" Fargo asked.

"Guess not, Fargo. Buffalo Wallow's promised to find me the perfect woman—and that's about what I need. He says I won't have to find gold with her takin' care of me." As he spoke, Charlie's eyes lit up in anticipation.

"Good luck, then."

"Same to you, Fargo."

Touching his hat brim in salute to his three friends, Fargo nudged his pinto forward, then lifted him quickly to a canter. A moment later, he entered the pine and began to lift into the mountains. He was heading back to Bent Rock. From there, he had no idea where he would go.

Unless, of course, he got lucky and came across Hawk Fletcher's trail once more.

Fargo took his time. His pinto needed to put some flesh back on, and Fargo needed more time to think. Besides, the Sawtooths were still alive with Comanches; so he rode very carefully and kept in the timber for most of his journey. But he rode steadily and a week and a half later arrived in Bent Rock a little after sundown.

Riding on through the town, he clopped across the small plaza, passed the church, and pulled up in front of Rita Mendoza's adobe hut. When he saw the blue lantern glowing in her window, he dismounted. Dropping the pinto's reins over the hitch rack in front of the hut, he mounted the low porch. His knock brought no reply. He knocked a second time.

"Who is it?" He recognized Rita's voice.

"Fargo."

The door opened and Rita was standing in the doorway, as beautiful as ever, but somehow a mite sadder. She looked as if she had forgotten how to laugh.

"I came a long way," he told her. "You going to invite me in?"

She stepped quickly aside. "Of course, Skye," she said apologetically. "You came so sudden. It is a surprise."

Stepping inside, he took off his hat. She closed the door, took his hat, and dropped it over a wooden peg in the wall beside the door. Then she led him into the kitchen. He sat down at the table while she fixed him coffee. They said little while she prepared it.

At last she sat down opposite him and poured coffee for both of them. Taking his cup, Fargo sipped it, then placed it down before him.

"Where's Pedro?" he asked.

She said nothing for a moment, then spoke, softly. "It was a long ride back. The wagon did not have an easy road. Pedro did not make it. I buried him in the Sawtooths."

"I'm sorry, Rita."

She leaned close. "Well, did you get him?"

"Hawk Fletcher?"

"You know who I mean."

154

"No."

She looked scornfully at him for a long moment. Then she shook her head. "Pedro and I, we travel so far. And now Pedro is dead. Now I must work in saloon so the men can fondle me. And after all this, that son of a bitch still lives."

She seemed about to cry. He reached out and took her hand. "Rita, we did what we could. We burned down Hell Town, killed most of his followers, and sent Fletcher packing. He's on the run now. At least we accomplished that much."

"You accomplished nothing! He will bring other men to him and rebuild his town. You must kill the head of the snake, not trample on his rattles."

Fargo sighed. He had tried to put a good face on it, but he agreed with Rita wholeheartedly. It was this truth—so clearly stated by Rita—that had been gnawing at him since he left Charlie and the others and began this long, lonely ride back to Bent Rock.

"Rita," he said warily, "I agree with you. That's why I left the others and rode back here. But I have one hope left. Have you seen any sign of Fletcher? If he wanted to start up again, this is where he'd come."

Her eyes focused suddenly in thought. "Yes, he come back here maybe," she said.

"Who does he know here?"

"Many."

"Any woman in particular?"

His question caused Rita's eyes to widen in excitement. "Fargo! You have say it! One week ago, Hawk Fletcher's woman returned to Bent Rock. I have not seen her. But this talk I hear in the saloon."

"What's her name?"

"Rosa de Sancha. Once she own saloon. But when Fletcher come by, she sell out to go off with him."

"But now she's back."

"Yes!"

"So that means Fletcher won't be far behind. Have you seen him?"

"No."

"Have you heard anything about him?"

"I hear nothing."

Fargo sipped his coffee intently, digesting what Rita had just told him.

Rita spoke softly. "I hear nothing, but maybe I see something."

He looked at her. "What?"

"Rosa, she live in top floor over Hanging Man Saloon. She own it once. When I see the girl bring up her meal, I notice something."

"Go on."

"She bring too much for one woman to eat. Rosa de Sancha is small woman. She does not eat all that food."

"You mean there's someone up there with her. Fletcher maybe? He could be the one helping her eat all that food."

She shrugged. "Is possible."

"Why would he hide like that?"

"Maybe he still afraid you come after him."

Fargo pondered that for a moment or two, then shrugged. "Maybe so."

"So now you see, Fargo! Now we get him! He is right in our trap."

"You think you could get more information, find out for sure if that's Hawk Fletcher up there?"

"Maybe I take up meal myself!"

"Do you think you could do that?"

"I will see tomorrow."

"Fine."

"And so now you can stay here with me. Sleep with me. I tell the men in saloon I have lover. They not insist I take them home. You mind?"

"Hell, no."

"Good. Now I make you fine meal. But first I fill tub with hot water so you be ready for me. While I cook, you scrub."

Fargo grinned. "It's a deal."

The meal made him sleepy. He went into Rita's room to wait for her to finish with cleaning the dishes, his mind foggy with sleep. He barely remembered his head hitting the pillow. When he awoke again, he was aware of her body alongside him, her back to him. She was asleep, breathing softly.

He was no longer tired, and her warmth pulled him closer to her. The smell of her hair was intoxicating. He rested his face in its luxuriant abundance and felt her stir and come awake. Reaching over, he cupped one of her breasts with his hand and felt its luminous warmth.

She scooted back eagerly against him, her buttocks pressing against his soaring erection. He tightened his hand on her breast and heard her sigh in pleasure. She lifted her arms and turned so they were facing each other, her lips inches from his.

"You are not too tired?" she asked, her voice husky with desire.

"What do you think?"

Her fingers closed about his shaft and she grunted in pleased surprise. "I do not think you are too tired."

He chuckled. "You sure there's nobody waiting to surprise me this time?"

"You must forgive me for that, Skye. Then I want only to trick you. Now all I want is you."

He kissed her on the lips, gently. "I forgive you."

She turned onto her back and opened her thighs. He lifted himself on top of her, and the last remnants of clinging sleep vanished as he felt her slender, lithe body under him. Swiftly, eagerly, she positioned herself, waiting for him to enter. Their lips touched, then opened, and her breath rushed out through her nostrils and brushed his cheek. As he plunged into her, she drew in a deep, gasping breath and slid her hands down his back, pushing him down and opening her thighs wider.

They both began thrusting hungrily. He cupped her hips in his hands, lifting her. She thrust eagerly up at him and dug her fingernails into his back. It was a sudden, careening urge to fulfillment for them both, as their bodies moved in a rapidly accelerating pace.

Too soon it was over.

She breathed heavily under him while she ran her fingers through his thick black hair. Gasping slightly for breath, he remained atop her, warmed by the crush of her breasts against his chest. She swallowed audibly and made a sound in her throat that he took for an expression of pleasure. Then she sighed, smiled up at him, and pulled her legs together under him.

He lifted himself off her and rolled onto his side, still facing her, one hand resting on her smooth hip. The musky smell of their lovemaking filled the small bedroom. Outside, the night was black and he could barely make out her pale face or the dark hollows from out of which her almond-shaped eyes gleamed at him.

"Are you finished?" she whispered softly, pressing herself toward him.

"No."

"Mmm, that's good. I am not finished, either."

He kissed her, not on the lips, but on the neck under her ear. She sighed and he gently moved his lips up to nibble on one of her earlobes. The searing intensity of a moment before was gone, to be replaced by a need to caress and be gentle, to feel her open before him like a flower to the sun, aware of the passion building slowly, truly within them both. He let his hand explore the warmth of her sumptuous breasts, his fingers flicking the upraised nipples delicately. Her long legs stirred and she began to moan softly.

Only then did he close his lips about hers. They softened, opened for his probing tongue, the sweet scent of her coming to him, inflaming him once more. Her hands had already found his reviving erection. Feverishly, she stroked him back to a thrusting rigidity.

Grabbing her hip, he pulled her hard against him. With no further hesitation, she raised her leg for him.

He thrust into her, then flowed over onto her once again, sinking deep into her fiery sheath. She was panting eagerly now as she closed her thighs and sucked him deep into her. Easing himself up onto his knees, he straddled her hips, going slowly wild with the feel of her squeezing him deep inside her.

Then she began to move again, this time with a slow, expert rotation of her hips. She dug her heels into his back and continued to move until a sudden shudder passed through her, and then another. She was coming, but he knew that was not all of it—that a part of her had still not been touched.

He, too, was unquenched, his throat aching with his need to empty himself completely into her.

Still clinging to him fiercely, she lay back, her eyes closed. A flush Fargo could see even in the dark suffused her face. He grasped her breast and felt its firm, silken smoothness come alive under his rough hand.

"Go deeper, Fargo. Deeper!"

Her aching urgency was as desperate as his. He lunged into her swiftly and fiercely, exulting in her sudden wild cry of pleasure. Arching his back above her, he slammed down with all his might, driving deep, impaling her on the bed, the flood building within him, forcing him to speed, to thrust. He felt himself reaching, reaching, building—and then he crested, like water over a high dam. He burst over, flooding Rita, engulfing her in his torrents.

He became only dimly aware of Rita's cries fading away to a long, sobbing moan—and then to a pleased, wondering exhaltation.

She lit cheroots for them both and they scooted up in the bed to smoke them. The excitement of what they had just experienced lingered in the air about them, filling them both with the contentment that comes only after such remorseless urgency has been satisfied . . . completely.

"I feel like I've been beaten up, squeezed, then hung out to dry," he told her.

"Me, too," she said, chuckling, her hand reaching to take his.

They smoked for a long while in perfect silence.

"Well," he said at length, stubbing out his cheroot, "I guess I can believe it now."

"Believe what?"

"This wasn't a trick."

Laughing, she punched him on the shoulder, then winced as her fist came against such unexpected solidity.

"You got any idea how we're going to work it tomorrow?"

"Yes."

"I'm listening."

"I will tell Pepita that I want to meet this famous woman. I will offer to bring up her dinner. It is a long climb with a very heavy tray, and she will be grateful."

"Suppose Rosa does not want any other girl to deliver her meals?"

"I will convince Pepita first, then explain to Rosa how sick is poor Pepita." Rita smiled brilliantly. "She is woman. She will understand what happen to us all every month, no?"

Fargo chuckled. "All right. Once you're up there—what, then?"

"I keep my eyes open. I can tell if man is with her. There is no woman can hide this. You will see."

"No, *you* will. Just be careful."

She put out her cheroot and snuggled close to him. "Of course I be careful," she told him, her voice slurred with sleep. "I not want to lose chance for more of what we have tonight."

He smiled in the darkness. After a moment, she was breathing softly, regularly, as sleep took her. He carefully lifted his arms from around her and looked down at her face, glowing softly against the pillow. It had been as good for her as it had for him, it seemed. And she didn't want to lose that.

Then he realized he must be getting soft. He felt the same way.

11

Peering out from under his hat brim, Fargo watched Rita lug the food tray into the Hanging Man Saloon and then head for the open stairs in back. A moment later she had vanished up the flight. Fargo pulled his whiskey closer and sipped it carefully. He had entered the saloon through the back door and taken a seat at a table about half an hour before. He hadn't known for sure if Rita had been able to convince Pepita to let her bring up Rosa's dinner.

Apparently, Rita had been successful. Now all Fargo had to do was restrain his impatience and wait for Rita to come back down and tell him if anyone who fit Hawk Fletcher's description was staying up there with Rosa.

Fargo was acutely aware that a number of Comancheros had escaped in addition to Hawk Fletcher. It was therefore sensible for Fargo to conclude that if the leader of the Comancheros was indeed upstairs with Rosa, those of his men who had escaped with him from Hell Town would not be far away.

The night's patrons were beginning to drift into the saloon by now, rapidly filling it with loud banter, cigar smoke, and the sound of grating chairs. Before long, the clink of poker chips could be heard from tables all around Fargo. Then the Mexican bar girls began drifting in and latching on to whichever patron caught their fancy. Bottoms were pinched and shrieks of feminine laughter filled the room. As Fargo sipped his whiskey and waited for Rita to come down, he was pleased that none of the girls bothered him. He did not think to wonder why this was so.

An hour later, Fargo was still waiting for Rita to come down.

Cold with anxiety by this time, he forced himself to wait another five minutes or so, then finished his drink and got to his feet. Only a few bothered to glance up at his big frame as he moved through the thick smoke to the back stairs. He was halfway up them when he noticed how silent—and watchful—those below him in the saloon had become.

He glanced down.

The saloon's patrons and the bar girls had moved silently back to the walls, and standing in the middle of the floor, their guns unholstered, were three grinning Mexicans, Comancheros by the look of them. They had been waiting for Fargo to make his move. Now it was their turn. As Fargo clawed for his six-gun, the three men, laughing at his surprise, began blasting up at him.

It was their drunken amusement that undoubtedly

saved Fargo. He flung himself flat on the stairs and returned their fire through the balusters, catching one of them in the gut and blowing a six-gun out of another man's hand. Then he raced on up the stairs, the rounds ripping through the balusters and into the walls above and behind him, showering him with plaster.

He kept going to the third floor, aware of the heavy boots pounding up after him. Once on the landing, he made for the nearest door. It was locked. He stepped back and kicked it open, then flung himself into the room—and found himself staring at Rita's bound and gagged figure. She was spread-eagled on her back on top of the blue silk coverlet of a large, canopied bed. Her face was swollen grotesquely and she was unconscious. Fargo saw tiny cuts on her neck, like the nicks of a fast-moving blade.

A door opened beside him and Hawk Fletcher stepped through the doorway, his pearl-handled revolver leveled on Fargo's gut. Behind him crouched the woman Fargo assumed was Rosa de Sancha.

"Drop the weapon, Fargo," Fletcher said.

Fargo tossed his Colt onto the bed.

"The knife too. Take it out real slow like and toss it alongside the revolver."

Fargo slipped the knife from its scabbard and did as Fletcher told him.

At that moment the sound of pounding feet filled the hallway as Fletcher's men raced up the stairway. A second later, they burst into the bedroom, guns drawn. There were only two of them. One had a red bandanna wrapped around his shattered gun hand.

"You all right, boss?" the first one demanded. It was clear to Fargo the gunman was not completely sober. The stench of whiskey hung like a cloak over him. This did not go unnoticed by Fletcher.

"What the hell does it look like?" Fletcher responded contemptuously. "A fine job you lushes did down there. How the hell could he have gotten past the three of you?"

"He blasted us," the man admitted. Then he added unhappily, "Miles is dead. Gut shot."

With a bitter curse, Fletcher glanced over at Fargo. "You're going to pay for this, you bastard."

"You want we should take him downstairs?" the first man asked.

"No, dammit! I'll handle this. Go on back down and sober up, both of you!"

The two men backed out of the room unhappily, like puppies who had just been scolded for messing on the carpet. When they were gone, Fletcher waggled his revolver at Fargo.

"Get into that living room," he told Fargo. "I want to look you over real good." He smiled. "Then I am going to kill you."

"Not here," Rosa breathed in some dismay.

Fletcher turned to her, his face suddenly dark with fury. "Get out of here, Rosa. I don't want you here no more!"

"But . . . this is my place!"

"And this is my gun," he told her in a voice so deadly Rosa quaked visibly.

She was a full-sized woman, as dark as Hawk Fletcher and almost as handsome. At the moment she was wearing only a loose-fitting nightgown that showed plenty of ankle. At Fletcher's command to leave, she snatched up her white fur robe and, tying the sash with quick, angry movements, turned and stalked from the room.

"Now, come in here," Fletcher told Fargo, waggling the Colt as he spoke.

"What did you do to this girl?" Fargo demanded.

Fletcher glanced in the bedroom at Rita and smiled coldly. "I worked her over some. What's that to you?"

Fargo left the bedroom and walked into the living room, Fletcher keeping him covered as he moved.

"Who the hell are you, anyway?" he demanded. "You wasn't just savin' that old fart back there in Hell Town, were you? And you two weren't just a couple of fools who wanted to join up with us. You been trackin' me. That girl in there, too. Some of it came out when I worked her over. Now I want to hear it. Tell me what this is all about."

"For me, it's about Conchita Alvarez."

Fletcher frowned in concentration then his eyes brightened. "Ah, sí," he said. "I remember that wildcat. She sleep with every man this side of the border. But me, she would not touch. A real bitch, that one!"

"So you burned her alive."

He was suddenly very pleased with himself. "I remember that. Yes. I burn her house and her barn. I sent her to hell with all the other whores."

Fargo hurled himself at Fletcher. But this time Fletcher was ready for him. Stepping deftly to one side, he brought the barrel of his Colt down on the back of Fargo's head, clubbing him to the thickly carpeted floor. As Fargo struck it, he felt the room tipping wildly under him; great, painful lights exploded deep inside his skull.

Turning his head he could see Fletcher bent over him, talking, but all Fargo could make out were dim, muffled sounds, like the buzzing of distant bees. He blinked up at Fletcher and tried to raise himself. The man smiled and stepped back, amused and pleased at Fargo's incapacity.

Closing his eyes, Fargo concentrated on regaining his senses. After a while the room came to a halt under him and once again presented his body with a solid, unyielding base. He opened his eyes carefully and stared straight ahead at the opposite wall. It trembled like a desert horizon for a moment, then grew still. Though his head was pounding painfully, Fargo was able to lift it up off the floor.

Fletcher was sitting in an upholstered chair, his Colt still covering Fargo.

"I have decided," Fletcher said, "to hang you. This night. It will be a great party. I will pay for the wine. And then all who see you twisting in the wind will know that Hawk Fletcher is no man to mess with. It will be a good lesson. After such a lesson, I will have no trouble getting more men—thanks to you, Fargo."

"Aren't you counting your chickens before they're hatched?"

"You mean you will stop me?"

"I mean I'm not dead yet."

"You will be."

"Then shoot me now. You won't drop any rope around my neck."

"Ah! That you not like eh? Good! What you not want, that is what I will do to you."

Fargo pushed himself to a sitting position. He was now less than five feet from Hawk Fletcher. And he was alone with him. If he waited much longer, any chance of him escaping would be impossible. Once he left the hotel, he would be encircled by the entire male population of Bent Rock, every one of them more than anxious to keep Fargo within Fletcher's grasp. This was a dull, isolated town. A lynching would break the monotony. There was nothing like hanging a man to bring a town like this together. It was better than a Fourth of July celebration.

So he had to act now.

He braced himself. At once Fletcher came alert. He raised his Colt, thumb-cocked it, and aimed carefully.

"Go ahead. Rush me. I won't kill you outright." He smiled. "I'll aim for something that'll cripple you without killing you—like an elbow or a knee."

Fargo sat back, his eyes on Fletcher, getting himself ready to spring.

Behind him, the bedroom door was flung open. Fargo saw quick surprise register on Fletcher's face. As he swung his Colt around and fired, his shot coincided with another blast from the doorway. Before Fletcher could fire again, Fargo flung himself on him.

Dropping his Colt, the man went back over the arm of the chair. His head hit the floor hard and Fargo dragged the groggy man to his feet and began punching at his face, ripping into his flesh with raking knuckles, driving him relentlessly back to the wall. Fletcher pawed back feebly, trying to ward off Fargo's

169

merciless barrage but Fargo was in another world now, punishing the man with a cold, steady, battering resolve until the only thing keeping him up was Fargo's fierce, unremitting flurry of punches.

At last, his breath coming in painful gasps, Fargo stepped back and let Fletcher—his face now resembling a side of raw beef—slide down the wall to the floor. Still panting heavily, Fargo looked stupidly down at his own bloody knuckles, then cautiously opened and closed his hands to make sure he could use them.

He could.

He bent and picked up Fletcher's pearl-handled Colt. Then, still breathing hard, he turned to look in the direction of the open bedroom door.

What he saw was like a punch in his stomach.

Rita was crumpled in the doorway, a steady river of blood streaming from her shattered midsection. In her hand was the Colt Fargo had thrown onto the bed. She must have used his knife to cut herself free when she regained consciousness. Coming to a halt over her, he saw the bloody lacerations left on her wrists from struggling with the knife.

He went down on one knee beside her, took his Colt gently from her grasp, then called her name softly. But there was no response. Nothing. A terrible chill fell over him.

Footsteps were pounding up the stairs again.

Fargo got to his feet and waited until the men reached the landing. Then he flung open the living-room door and emptied his Colt at two men, the same two who had come up earlier.

As the rounds pumped into them, they dropped their guns and staggered back. One collapsed in the hallway, the other managed to scramble back to the head of the stairs and begin a punishing, panicky flight down the stairwell. Fargo leaned over the banister, sighted quickly on the man's head, and fired. The bullet went clear through his skull, spattering the opposite wall and some of the stairs with brains and pieces of his skull. The gunman came to rest with what was left of his face staring back up at Fargo.

Fargo returned to Rosa de Sancha's living room and closed the door.

He lifted the still-dazed and battered Hawk Fletcher from the floor, stepped over Rita's dead body, and carried Fletcher over to the bed, where he dumped him. Scattered over the coverlet were several pieces of the rope Rita had cut through. Fargo selected appropriate lengths and bound Fletcher's wrists and ankles, then attached them to the head-board and foot of the bed so that Fletcher was forced to lay spread-eagled on the silk coverlet. Then Fargo emptied the kerosene contents of the room's two lamps onto the bed, not forgetting to drench Fletcher's body thoroughly.

That done, he went into the next room and picked up two more lamps, emptying the contents of one over the floor and the contents of the other against the walls, saturating the walls from floor to ceiling. By this time the smell of kerosene in the room was overpowering. He found some wooden sulfur matches in one of the bed stands and stepped back toward the door.

That was when Hawk Fletcher shook himself out of his stupor and gazed over at Fargo. When he realized how snugly he was bound, he moistened his swollen lips. "What'n hell you up to?" he gasped.

"You burned Conchita alive. I promised her I'd see you went the same way."

The man's eyes widened in sudden, abject terror. "No! Listen to me, Fargo! I have silver mines! Millions. I can make you a rich man!"

Fargo shook his head. "No, Fletcher." He struck a match and held it out over the floor.

"I'll do anything! Anything you say!"

"All I want you to do is think about Conchita and what you said just now—about sending her to hell with all the other whores." Fargo smiled. "If she's in hell, mister, you'll meet her soon enough."

"No! For God's sake, Fargo!"

"No, Fletcher. For Conchita's sake—and all the others you raped and pillaged."

Fargo tossed the match to the floor. The kerosene-saturated rug burst immediately into flame, an enormous sheet of it flashing between Fargo and the bed. Backing out swiftly, Fargo pulled the door shut, turning the bedroom into a furnace. The mounting roar within the bedroom was almost loud enough to drown out Fletcher's screams.

Almost.

With Rita's body in his arms, his Colt fully loaded, Fargo picked his way down the stairs past the dead man staring up at eternity. When he reached the saloon, he found it empty. Only the barkeep was in sight, crouched behind the bar. He was reaching for his shotgun when Fargo shifted Rita's body and fired at him. The mirror behind him shattered and the man dived for cover.

"Stay down," Fargo told him, "and you just might live."

He crossed the empty floor and pushed out through the batwings, coming to a halt on the porch. Four Comancheros—Hawk Fletcher's backup men—were waiting for him across the street, their feet wide, their six-guns in their hands.

"Look up at the top floor," Fargo told them.

They did as he bid, and saw the smoke and flames pouring out of the windows. From where Fargo was standing, he couldn't see the flames, but he could smell and hear the dull roar of the flames as they fought their way out of the bedroom and swept into the living room.

"Hawk Fletcher's up there," Fargo shouted across to the four men. "On his way to hell! You can join him if you want."

"You can't shoot all of us."

'I don't intend to try. If I get just one more of you bastards, that'll be comfort enough for me."

The four men hesitated. It dawned on them that not all of them were going to emerge from this alive, and from where they stood, they could see the flames that were now devouring their leader.

But they were as obstinate as they were stupid.

First one, then the other three raised their Colts.

Fargo flung himself flat on the porch just as the four opened up. As the hot lead slammed into the steps beside him, Fargo returned their fire and saw one of them stagger to his knees and blow a hole in the ground before toppling onto his side.

A bullet slammed into Fargo's left upper forearm. He cursed and squeezed off another shot—just as someone with a rapid-fire rifle opened up on the Comancheros from farther down the street. The fire was withering, and the three men stumbled back in their eagerness to escape the fusillade. Fargo immediately added his two cents—and that did it.

Holstering their six-guns, the remaining three Comancheros vaulted into their saddles and galloped off down the street. The fusillade followed them a ways, then gave up.

Fargo got to his feet and picked up Rita's body, then darted down the steps and away from the hotel, for by then the flaming embers were breaking through the windows and it appeared as if the entire roof was ablaze. Somewhere a bell was tolling wildly, and by the time Fargo reached the other side of the street, a bucket brigade was already forming up.

Fargo examined his wound. It was bleeding cleanly and giving him little discomfort. He was satisfied it was only a flesh wound. Glancing down the street in the direction from which the gunfire had come, he saw Charlie Kettle drive his wagon out of an alley and head down the street toward him. His Henry was resting across his knee, and he waved when he saw Fargo had caught sight of him.

*　　*　　*

174

Two days later, after Rita had been given a decent burial, Fargo left Bent Rock with Charlie Kettle, riding up on the seat beside the old-timer, his pinto tied to the tailgate. The two men had gone a considerable distance before Fargo cleared his throat and turned to Charlie.

"You've been refusing to tell me," Fargo said, "but I won't let you hold off any longer. How come you showed up in Bent Rock looking for me? Not that I'm not grateful, mind. But hell, the last I knew, you and Buffalo Wallow were on your way to meeting a Ute woman who was going to make your life a heaven on earth—or something like that."

Charlie spat a gob of tobacco juice at a pink wildflower along the trace. He caught it dead center. "Her name was Willow Tree, a fine woman, Skye. I won't deny that."

"So?"

"And she was Buffalo's sister."

"I figured as much."

Charlie chewed his cud awhile longer, contemplating, then let fly with another gob of tobacco. "I don't need to tell you what that big Indian looks like."

"No, you don't."

"Well, by grannies, Fargo, you can strike me dead if I ain't tellin' the truth—Willow Tree looked just like him."

Fargo tried to imagine it. And when he was able to conjure in his mind's eye Buffalo Wallow's dark, round face, the obsidian eyes, and the powerful hulking body wrapped in a squaw's deerskin dress, he began to laugh. Then Charlie started to laugh too.

When they reached their campsite four hours later, the two men were still laughing.

LOOKING FORWARD!

**The following is the opening section
from the next novel in the exciting
Trailsman Series from Signet:**

The Trailsman #47

SIX-GUN SALVATION

*In 1860, just above Farewell Bend in the
new state of Oregon, where some
came to steal and some came to save,
and the Northern Shoshoni arrows
made no distinction . . .*

"I'm getting the hell out of here," the big man with the
lake-blue eyes muttered.

"You most certainly are not, Mr. Fargo," the Rev.
Joshua Johnston hissed. Fargo threw a grimace of
exasperation at the man as the reverend leaned forward in the saddle, his long-tailed, black minister's
coat making him look like a huge crow on the horse.
Rev. Johnston's long, lean face gazed down at the lone
wagon rolling across the hollow of land. Fargo's eyes

flickered to the line of near-naked bronzed horsemen in the distant timber as they paralleled the wagon below.

"That Conestoga is going to be attacked," the minister said.

"By fifteen Northern Shoshonis. Those are no-win odds, and I'm getting out of here," Fargo said.

"No, you're not. It's your Christian duty to help the people in that wagon down there," Rev. Johnston said, his long, lean face growing longer and leaner with righteousness.

"Where does the bible say a Christian has to be a damn fool?" Fargo threw back.

The Rev. straightened his spare, bony frame and clutched the small, black leatherbound bible to his chest. "A Christian feels a responsibility to his fellow man," he intoned.

"I feel a responsibility to my scalp," Fargo snapped. Rev. Johnston turned his eyes back to the Conestoga that rolled through the hollow. "You coming?" Fargo speared.

"I am not. I am going down there to give those people whatever help I can," the minister answered.

"You can't help them, dammit. All you can do is get your hide shot full of Shoshoni arrows. It's suicide," Fargo said.

The minister shot a glance of something close to pity at the big man. "You just can't understand the power of faith, can you, Mr. Fargo? Believing will protect me. Believing, that's what matters. What do you believe, Mr. Fargo?" the minister said.

"I believe there are too damn many idiots in this world, and I'm not going to make one more," Fargo growled. "That Conestoga down there, one wagon alone out here, that's being idiotic."

"Perhaps they trust in the Lord, too. Perhaps they believe, too, Fargo," Rev. Johnston answered.

"They won't be the first ones he's disappointed," Fargo returned, and saw the minister's eyes grow wide with shock.

"That's blasphemy," the minister breathed.

"No, the Lord doesn't reward stupidity. That's been proven plenty of times," Fargo said. Fargo glanced at the Shoshoni again. The Indians continued to filter through the trees like silent shadows, unaware they were being watched, their concentration on the lone Conestoga below. Suddenly, as one, the fifteen loin-clothed riders turned their ponies and began to drift downward.

"The Shoshoni have stopped watching. So have I," Fargo said.

The reverend's eyes stayed on the wagon below as the Shoshoni came out of the timber and into plain view. "They must see those savages now," the minister murmured. "But they just keep rolling on at the same pace."

"It's hard to make a cirle with one wagon," Fargo observed, and bitterness laced his words. "For the last time, you coming or do you like watching a massacre?" Fargo said.

The cry from the Shoshoni swept away the reverend's answer, and as Fargo started to send the Ovaro upward into the high timber, he saw the Indians racing their shot-legged ponies downhill. He glimpsed rifle barrels being poked out from under the canvas of the Conestoga and saw the driver climb inside the body of the wagon. He heard the rifles bark, old single-shot weapons for the most part, and he watched the streaking cluster of Shoshoni peel away from one another like a sunflower peeling back its leaves. Fargo continued to look back as the Ovaro climbed the hillside. He cursed as his view was momentarily obscured by long black coattails flapping across his gaze. Rev. Johnston was riding full tilt down the hill to the wagon, which had come to a stop.

"Dammit to hell," Fargo swore as he reined up in a cluster of black oak. The reverend had almost reached the wagons, firing a big Dragon Colt with a hell of a lot more righteousness than accuracy at the line of Shoshoni that raced around the wagon in a furious circle.

"Heathens," Fargo heard the reverend shout. "Savage heathens."

The Shoshoni answered with an arrow that struck him right between the shoulder blades, and the minister twisted in the saddle before he fell from the horse. He landed only a dozen feet from the wagon and started to crawl toward the undercarriage when another arrow hit him, this one in the small of his back. The minister twitched in pain, lay still for a moment, and then continued to try to pull himself under the Conestoga.

"Ah, shit," Fargo swore as he slid out of the saddle and yanked the big Sharps from its saddle case. He saw the bottom edge of the canvas pulled up on the Conestoga as a man leaned out, reached down to grab hold of the minister. He stayed that way as three arrows hurtled through him to pin him to the side of the wagon, head down. A woman screamed, came half out to try to pull the man back. The arrow that plunged halfway through her abdomen knocked her back into the wagon.

Fargo knelt down as he drew the Colt and held the rifle in his other hand. There was only one chance, he realized. It had worked, more often than not, and when it didn't, you ran like hell. He fired two shots from a big Sharps, two from the Colt, another two from the rifle and then two more fired simultaneously.

He saw the circling Shoshoni look up toward the hill where he lay as they continued their circling. He reloaded, moved a half-dozen steps to his right, fired a volley from the Colt and another from the rifle, again.

The reverend had crawled under the Conestoga, he saw, as the Shoshoni broke off their attack on the wagon but stayed apart to make themsleves harder targets. But he was firing for effect, not accuracy, and he blasted another volley off with the rifle.

He had counted on a basic element of the Indian, and it was working, he saw with grim satisfaction. Fearless in battle, the Indian was an instinctive tactician, always wary of being drawn into a trap by what he couldn't see, the caution ingrained in war between the tribes.

Fargo watched as one of the bucks, a young figure wearing a golden-eagle feather in his browband, waved an arm and peeled away. The others followed at once, still leaving plenty of distance between one another. The Shoshoni rode into the trees of the slope at the other side of the hollow, and Fargo watched as they made their way upward. He allowed a sigh of relief to escape his lips. They hadn't been a war party, painted up for killing on the outside and charged with it on the inside. They'd not have broken off, not this quickly. They'd been a hunting party that saw an easy mark and descended on it. But their real reason for going on had been the one echoed by the wagon as Fargo brought his gaze to focus on it. It resembled a giant pincushion on wheels. The Shoshoni had done what they'd set out to do. There'd be one less band of settlers, and they were content with that much.

Fargo stayed in place as he watched the movement of the leaves on the opposite hill and traced the Shoshoni's path over the crest. He waited further, though, watched to see if they changed their minds and circled back. But the distant foliage remained still. He rose, holstered the guns, and climbed onto the Ovaro. He sent the magnificent black-and-white-marked horse streaking downhill, out into the open land and toward the wagon. Maybe someone was still alive, still crouched in frozen fear. Maybe even Rev. Johnston, he grunted, and knew that the word maybe mocked probability.

He leapt from the horse as he reached the wagon and went to the rear of the Conestoga to peer through the elliptical opening in the canvas. He felt his jaw tighten as he saw three people, one man and two women, all dead. They and the man pinned to the side of the wagon had been the only occupants. No children, he noted, and felt grateful for that much. He always felt that way when there were no children. They were the innocents, the real victims. He stared for a moment at the three figures sprawled among the cloth satchels and bags that were their only worldly possessions, and stepped back, went around to the side of the wagon, and dropped down to one knee to peer underneath.

Rev. Johnston lay on his side, a third arrow protruding from between his ribs. But Fargo heard the sound of rasped breathing. He reached in, pulled the minister out between the wheels. He looked at the three arrows, all deeply embedded, and wondered that the man was still alive. Then he saw the minister's eyes open. The reverend stared at him for a long moment, and his hand slowly lifted to fasten itself around Fargo's arm. "You . . . go on, Fargo," the man said, each word a hollow rasp. "You paid . . . go on.

Tell the others . . . tell Leah. She will lead now . . . tell her."

"Leah?" Fargo repeated.

The minister's eyes blinked a nod. "Leah . . . Sister . . ." he breathed.

"Your sister?" Fargo asked.

"Sister of the Church . . . servant . . . servant of the Lord . . . righteous woman," the reverend gasped out. "Leah . . . all in her hands now. You go with Leah, Fargo." Fargo felt the man's hand tighten on his arm for a brief instant, then fall away as the minister's body sagged. The effort had drained what little life there was left in Rev. Johnston, and Fargo let the man's limp form slide to the ground.

"Damn," Fargo bit out as he stood up and his eyes swept the distant hillside out of habit. But only the swoop of a pair of tanagers broke the stillness. His mouth was a hard, thin line, he forced himself not to just ride away, which is what the anger inside him pushed at him. He unhitched the two horses, tethered them on a single, long lead. They'd bring a fair price somewhere. He found a shovel hanging from the tailgate of the Conestoga and began the digging. The ground was soft, and he dug a wide grave, cursing with each shovelful of earth as the anger stayed inside him. When he finished he'd buried the three dead travelers and the reverend, bible on his chest, and stood before the wide, flat mound. The anger was a hard rock in the pit of his stomach. No words of solace or piety came to him, and the only words he found welled up out of the anger inside him. "I was right," he said accusingly as he stared at the far left of the wide mound where he'd placed Rev. Joshua Johnston. "He doesn't reward stupidity. Amen."

Fargo strode away, climbed onto the Ovaro, and rode north at a fast trot, pulling the two horses from the wagon behind him. He slowed when the hollow widened, became a small plain dotted with clusters of gambel oaks. The town of Farewell Bend lay only a few miles north, he estimated. That's where the reverend had been headed with him when they'd spotted the lone Conestoga. The town's name held a grim appropriateness, Fargo grunted, and his lips pulled back in disgust. The thought of riding trail for some dried-up, pinch-faced, righteous, lecturing old spinster was a lot less than appealing. In fact, he had almost turned down the reverend when the man sought him out up in Sweetbridge. Fargo's lips stayed drawn back as the meeting drifted through his mind. He had brought Tom Ingraham's wife and two boys over the Salmon River Mountains across Idaho to Sweetbridge, and he and Tom had celebrated for two days and nights. But he'd sobered and was preparing to leave when the reverend came up to him.

"I am Rev. Joshua Johnston, a minister of the Church of the Word," the man had said as he introduced himself. "You are Fargo, the Trailsman."

Fargo recalled tossing the minister a narrow-eyed stare. "They call me that," he had answered cautiously. "You come recruiting, you're wasting your time, Reverend."

"I've come on business, Fargo," Rev. Johnston had said. "I want you to take me and my followers into the Painted Hills territory."

"Where into the Painted Hills?" he'd questioned.

"I'll tell you as we go along," the reverend had said.

"No dice, preacher, when I break trail, I want to know where, what, and why," Fargo said.

"All right, I'll give you the details when we get to Farewell Bend. My followers are waiting there for me," the minister had said.

"What kind of followers?" Fargo asked.

"Men, women, families, all believers. You can call them my disciples, apostles. We are all missionaries. We want to bring the Word to everyone, especially the heathen savages."

"They've already got their word. They'll take a lot of convincing," Fargo remarked.

"Faith, believing, will show me the way to them," Rev. Johnston had answered, and Fargo remembered shrugging. The reverend had a right to try, he had muttered silently. He wasn't the first to do so, and it was likely he wouldn't be the last. But sensing rejection, the minister had named his price to be paid in advance, and it had been the kind of money hard to turn down. But it had really been the letter from Tom Haydon's widow in his pocket that had decided him to take the job. Jessie had written of how desperately she needed money to save the farm back in Kansas since

Tom died. He'd had the letter in his mind when he took the reverend's offer.

Fargo gave a harsh grunt as he rode. He had sent the money to Jessie on the first post. There was no way for him to give it back and bow out. He had to go through with it, and he shook his head angrily at the thought. But a man had to live by his own rules, and fair was fair.

He continued north, and the day began to move toward dusk when he caught sight of the town. He sent the Ovaro into a canter, pulled the two wagon horses behind him, and slowed again when he rode into Farewell Bend. The town surprised him by being larger than he'd expected, containing a bank and a meeting hall as well as a dance hall. Deciding not to waste time searching for the reverend's followers, he halted at the town blacksmith shop.

"Mighty fine-looking horse," the smithy said with the eye of a man who knew his horseflesh.

"Thanks," Fargo nodded. "You see any church folks in town? I think there's likely to be a fair-size group."

"Sounds like those at Emmet's Boarding Hotel," the blacksmith said. "Last house other end of town."

"Obliged," Fargo said, and moved the Ovaro on through Farewell Bend. The boarding hotel was indeed the last structure of the town, he saw as he reached it, a large, two-story clapboard building painted yellow with white trim. He halted and took in the collection of wagons that were drawn up on both sides of the house: two proper Conestogas, a high-sided Bucks County hay wagon outfitted with a canvas top, two Owensboro seed-bed wagons built with wooden bows for canvas tops, a big California rack-bed wagon with sides and roof of thin wood built on, and a milk wagon painted light green and with curtains on the windows. He grimaced, dismounted, and went into the boarding hotel.

A huge figure, nearly three hundred pounds, Fargo guessed, leaned against one wall inside the entrance. A mountainous, overstuffed belly strained against a white sleeveless shirt to the breaking point. Above it, huge shoulders made a fat face seem small despite its folds of flesh and hanging jowls and bald pate. Fargo saw the mountain of flesh watch him until he turned and went down a wide hallway to knock on the first door.

He heard footsteps behind the door, and then the latch turned and the door pulled open. He found himself staring at a young woman. A cascade of blond hair framed a face as sensual as it was georgeous, full, very red lips, the lower one slightly thicker than the upper; both finely molded at the edges; a short, straight nose; cream-white skin; and deep-blue eyes that absolutely smoldered. The rest of her matched the face, he noted. A gray dress of determined plainness might well have been a red satin gown on her figure as it clung to magnificently curved, full breasts, narrowed quickly to a small waist, and rested on long, slowly curving thighs, a figure that sent contained sensualness in waves.

"Yes?" she asked, and the deep-blue eyes somehow managed to be cool as they smoldered.

"Excuse me, I think I've got the wrong place," Fargo apologized.

"Perhaps you have the right place for the Lord's Word is here," she said, and Fargo felt his eyebrows lift.

"It is?" he said. "I'm looking for Leah."

"I'm Leah," the gorgeous creature answered.

Fargo felt his eyebrows go higher. "Holy shit," he heard himself mutter, and wondered if he should add hallelujah. He saw a tiny layer of frost come over the smoldering eyes. "It's just that you're not what I expected," he said.

The tiny smile that parted the full, red lips held both tolerance and an edge of superiority. "Surprises are good for us. They teach us caution," she said.

"Guess so," he murmured, and decided that the throbbing sensuality was tightly held under wraps. Probably damn well had to be, he told himself.

"Have you come to inquire about the Church?" Leah asked.

"I've come about Rev. Johnston," he said.

Her smile widened. "The reverend is due back today. He is our leader, you know," she said.

"Was your leader," Fargo corrected.

She caught the note in his voice, and the smoldering eyes clouded. "What do you mean?" She frowned.

"I mean he ran himself into a handful of Shoshoni arrows," Fargo said.

Shock leapt in the deep-blue eye as she stared back. "How do you know this?" she questioned.

"I was with him. Name's Fargo . . . Skye Fargo," he said.

"You're the one he went to Sweetbridge to hire, the Trailsman," Leah said. Fargo nodded, and she pulled the door open wider, leaned back, and called into the room. "Mishach. Shadrach," she called. "Did you hear?"

The two men appeared from behind the door, each with a rifle pointed at him. "We heard," one said as the young woman stepped back. "Get in here, mister," he ordered.

𝒟

xciting Westerns by Jon Sharpe

Prices higher in Canada

**Buy them at your local
bookstore or use coupon
on next page for ordering.**

SIGNET Brand Westerns You'll Enjoy